Voices from a Time

Voices from a Time

A NOVEL

Silvia Bonucci

TRANSLATED BY MARTHA KING

WINNER OF THE ZERILLI-MARIMÒ PRIZE

STEERFORTH ITALIA

AN IMPRINT OF STEERFORTH PRESS · HANOVER, NEW HAMPSHIRE

First published in Italian by Edizioni e/o, Rome, 2003

Voices from a Time is winner of the Zerilli-Marimò Prize for Italian Fiction, sponsored by New York University and the Fondazione Maria and Goffredo Bellonci. Funding is made possible by Baroness Zerilli-Marimò, as well as through contributions from Casa della Letterature in Italy. The publishers would like to thank Baroness Zerilli-Marimò for her support of this publication.

The epigraph on page vii was translated by Robert Harrison and reprinted from *Umberto Saba: An Anthology of His Poetry and Criticism*, Troy, Michigan: International Book Publishers, 1986.

For information about permission to reproduce
selections from this book, write to:
Steerforth Press L.C., 25 Lebanon Street
Hanover, New Hampshire 03755

Library of Congress Cataloging-in-Publication Data

Bonucci, Silvia, 1964-
[Voci un tempo. English]
Voices from a time : a novel / Silvia Bonucci ;
translated by Martha King. — 1st ed.
   p.cm.
ISBN-13: 978-1-58642-098-7 (alk. paper)
ISBN-10: 1-58642-098-4 (alk. paper)
1. Jews — Italy — Trieste — Fiction. I. King, Martha, 1928– II. Title.

PQ4902.O67V6313 2006
853'.92—dc22

2005029900

Voices from a Time is a work of fiction, based on real family characters now deceased.
Any resemblance between these and actual living persons is purely coincidental.

FIRST EDITION

To Grandmother, because this is her story.
And to Father, who didn't make it in time to read it . . .

Dear discordant voices from the past,
come back to me!
Who knows in what new sweeter melody
I yet may make you resonate?

Umberto Saba
from "Preludio e fughe"

MARCELLO

DOLLY

*M*ARCELLO WAS BORN in Trieste in 1898, two years before me.

One of my earliest memories of the two of us is in Cairo. It was probably 1903. I can still see the lush garden of a colonial villa, dust and blinding light. And then an English governor, a ball rolling down dark cellar steps, and the authoritarian voice that ordered me to go get it. I can still remember refusing to obey, terrorized by that darkness. My fear, my tears, my terror, and Marcello, five years old, who offers in vain to go in my place.

We were in Cairo because of Father. The bank had sent him to head the branch in the Egyptian capital for a few years. From that period I still have three photographs: one of me alone, one with Marcello, and another on camels in front of the pyramids and Sphinx. Obviously this last one is the most picturesque, so absurd in its setting, with those ladies from Trieste on camels, I in Father's arms, and Marcello in a big straw hat sitting tranquilly on a dromedary crouched in the center of a group of Bedouins. The developer of the photographs is the Atelier Reiser, Photographie Artisque, Alexandrie et Le Caire (Egypte). On the back of each print, on the lower left, always the same inscription: *les clichés sont conservés*.

❖

I believe we returned to Trieste toward the end of 1905. We arrived at our villa by carriage early in the evening. Torches had been lit along the stairs and the servants were lined up waiting for us. Marcello, anxious and nervous, sat next to me. I remember Father scolding him because he kept tapping on the window. When we left the carriage to go into the house, Mama looked radiant and almost ran to the door. The servants bowed, and I only saw their feet protruding from black skirts and trousers. Then something happened, because Mama turned her frightened face to me: "Where is Marcello?" I looked at her in surprise: where did she think he would be? Here, next to me . . . But no, he wasn't. He had disappeared. They looked for him everywhere: signorino here, signorino there. I never did find out where he went to hide.

In Trieste my mother, Gemma, was reunited with her ephemeral society world, the large group of admirers that Father called her "court." I remember the parties, the balls, the colors, and the rustle of absurdly elaborate dresses. Marcello and I often hid behind the banisters of the center stairs to spy on our parents in evening dress as they were ready to leave. Gemma always had a triumphant air and Marcello observed her in silence, apprehensive and vigilant, before inevitably turning to me to whisper: "Did you see how beautiful Mama is?"

For maybe I haven't already said so: my mother's beauty was almost offensive.

However, Mama was practically never home. And when she was, her presence became — how to put it — overflowing.

Sometimes she would erupt into the house with her latest purchases and would get Marcello and me to come watch while she tried things on. She extracted from big boxes hats, dresses, capes that she showed off with poses and simpering ways to make us laugh. Other times she had us get all dressed up and took us to the fair to eat cotton candy. "I can't go there alone," she would say. "You know what a bad impression that would make!" She also liked to go to the Old Town, where there were mussel vendors, or *mussoleres*, as she called them, who knew her and pretended to be pleased by her peculiarity. When she saw one of them on a street corner she would tap merrily on the window for the carriage to stop. Then she would hurriedly descend, buy three paper cones *de mussoli*, and take off her gloves before devouring the mussels one after the other: "Careful 'cause the paper's all greasy!"

During those years, because we were constantly moving, Marcello and I went from one tutor to another — Germans, French, men, women, young, old . . . it was difficult to follow a coherent program in all that, and I imagine that our education suffered from it. This didn't bother us as much as the fact that we were often in the hands of ill-prepared and authoritarian people. My basically apathetic character adapted to this situation with relative ease, but it was different for Marcello. By the time he was eight years old my brother was already showing signs of a very strong personality, difficult to sway and little inclined to accept the adults' world without argument, as one should then. It was a little as though he were going through an adolescent crisis prematurely. I was too young to understand certain aspects of his behavior, but I was fascinated by it and would have liked to have resembled him at least a little. The relationship with our tutors only got worse and my parents decided to separate us and entrust us to different teachers, in the hope that I at least might learn something and that my mind would not be contaminated by my brother's subversive spirit.

However, what my parents never knew was that Marcello would come to my room after the lessons to go over everything in his own way.

"What did you do today?"

"The tutor told me a fable by La Fontaine."

"But hasn't he taught you to read yet?"

"I'm too little, and besides I'm a girl . . ."

"Excuse me, what did you say?"

"Mama says there's no hurry for girls, because it doesn't do much good for girls to study a lot."

"Sometimes Mama says foolish things. You have to study if you want to become a person."

"You mean get big?"

"A person, I said, no matter if big or small."

When Marcello got sick we were in Milan and the medical diagnosis left little room for hope: "meningococcal meningitis." Although I was still a child, that period made an impression on me. I learned nothing specifically from the moment I was strictly forbidden to go into Marcello's room, but what I saw in the house was enough to make me understand that something more serious was going on than what my parents wanted me to know.

I was convinced that Marcello would die and I bothered my poor father with absurd questions that only children know how to ask. "If Marcello dies will I get another little brother?"

"Dolly, Marcello is not dying. Stop talking like that and go to your room to review the poem."

"I've already done that. Do you want me to recite it?"

"Not now. I have to go see Marcello."

"I'll come, too. I'll recite it to him. Marcello likes to hear me recite poetry . . ."

"Not now, Dolly, he is too tired. Another time . . ."

Another time. I heard those words for weeks — weeks during which I went from one servant to another without ever getting a real explanation. Always a bother, always in the way, by now almost envious of all the attention my brother received.

During his convalescence I could spend a few hours in the afternoon with Marcello, sometimes in his room, sometimes on the veranda where the servants brought him when there was a little sun.

My brother had taken up drawing, and he loved to hear me recite poetry while he made some rapid sketch. He asked for news about Beppina, my favorite doll, and tirelessly related the story of the Count of Monte Cristo, especially the second part, about the vendetta. He was still weak and in pain, but he had the attentive look of someone who missed nothing. Every once in a while he would straighten up in his armchair and in his nasal voice intone a Triestine song:

When the sea is rough
and the waves are wild
Teresina falls in love
Teresina falls in love
When the sea is rough
and the waves are wild
Teresina falls in love . . .

It was one of Mama's favorite songs, and Marcello always hoped to hear her slightly hoarse voice conclude from a distance: "With a poor fisherman!"

The truce with his illness was short. After a little more than a year, Marcello began to have unbearable headaches. However, that year was a very intense time for the two of us, during which we became inseparable. On the long afternoons that we spent together after the lessons we invented all kinds of things: from Greek tragedies to marionettes, from Chinese shadows to poetry contests. We dressed up in costumes. Marcello created original dramatizations. We ravaged the classic texts. We created imaginary characters. I still have some photos, taken at a later time, that show me along with Marcello and one of my friends in theatrical poses: our first attempt at a photo story . . . Actually, of all those artistic ventures, the theater was the only one we kept up over the years. Because, if Marcello never completely abandoned poetry and drawing, after the headaches began he devoted himself to it in a very different way: they became his alone, a solitary exercise.

He also began to hide and was able to disappear for hours, in the carriage garage or in the attic or in some secret room. I almost always knew where he was, and I also knew he went there to be quiet, to write and draw things that he would show me surreptitiously later because no one liked them. Mama and the tutors would question me, sometimes crossly, but I never revealed his hiding places: I would never have broken the pact of loyalty that bound us.

Mornings, after breakfast, when the nanny took us to Mama for her kiss and clothes inspection, we almost always found her at her dressing table in her negligee busily brushing her hair. Mama took care of her complicated coiffure herself and had perfected a technique all her own to dominate that thick and splendid head of hair. She used three brushes corresponding to different stages of the lengthy operation. The first brush, with soft and wide bristles, served to unsnarl the knots more slowly. Once this was done she passed to brush number two, more compact and penetrating, to finally finish — when her hair now gave no resistance — with brush number three. I, who had to struggle daily with my frizzy black hair, envied her soft luminous hair and watched her admiringly from the door, unable to go near that body so haughtily draped in a dressing gown.

"Why stand there like a statue . . . Come on in! If you'd like you can brush my hair a little." When she was in a good mood, Mama would let Marcello or me collaborate in the third stage. To make it easier for us she would sit on a lower stool and lean her head back. Then her hair would almost reach the floor and the unnatural position made her chest lightly pulsate. I remember the shiver of emotion that ran over my hand when it was my turn, and my fear of hurting her, and my brother's expression as he watched me carefully, ready to replace me at Mama's first grimace of pain.

A couple of years after Marcello's recovery we moved to Paris, on Rue Récamier. It was there that Giorgio, nicknamed Titti, was born, my youngest brother. The birth of that splendid baby almost made Gemma forget she had two other children. Not that she had paid a whole lot of attention before, but after Giorgio's arrival her disinterest became nearly absolute. It is true that Marcello, so melancholy, fragile, and homely, couldn't compete with Titti's radiant beauty. As for myself, I had become very fat following a banana-based diet a doctor prescribed for me to regain my strength after breaking a leg, and besides I had never aroused any special feeling of tenderness in Gemma.

And so life for Marcello became even more complicated. It was complicated by a germ that had invaded his mind for some time, a sick and unrequited love, an inextinguishable torment that kept him even from looking his mother in the face, because he knew how dangerous his intense and passionate look was . . . My parents obstinately refused to think it was something that went well beyond the headaches and the aftermath of his illness. A seed planted long ago, which had found such fertile ground it could sprout nearly undisturbed.

Shortly after Titti was born, Marcello became even more intolerant and possessive where Gemma was concerned. Every time he saw her come in the door he made her account for her activities. He wanted to know the names of the people she had seen, how long she had stayed, what she wore. Moreover, when my parents went out together in the evening, Marcello fell into a restless state of which I was the only and inevitable victim.

He would come into my room with a book, sit on the sofa near the window, and wait: "Do you mind if I stay here and read for a little while? Only long enough to finish this chapter . . ." He frantically sought company during those times of anxiety, almost as though he was frightened by what he might do if left alone. I loved his visits, because even if he often didn't say a word, I felt he needed me. I tried to get him involved in my games, in my fantasies, and in the beginning he would make an effort to please me, because he was good-hearted and didn't want to let me down. But I realized he was somewhere else, far away, and I suffered from his suffering because I didn't understand it and felt unable to help him.

I don't know who was the first to speak to Gemma about the work of that "strange Viennese doctor" — to use Mama's childlike phrase — nor do I understand today what gave her the idea to try such an unorthodox method. My father, as usual, stayed on the sidelines when it came to family matters, but I presume that his desire for peace was so strong that he would accept anything.

Not that Marcello showed violent tendencies or refused to study. Quite the opposite. He was an exceptionally intelligent child, so brilliant as to sometimes cause amazement and worry. If he did not readily submit to discipline it was never out of pure rebellion, but rather from excessive analysis. He could take nothing as a given; everything had to be discussed and demonstrated with patience, and the more complicated the reasoning, the more inclined he was to accept it. Perhaps I was the only one who understood that what many called his "arrogance" was only an exasperated form of melancholy, an inner sadness that kept him from laughing, from letting himself go freely, from simply being a child. It's not accidental that when I remember the Marcello of those days I always see an adult caged in a boy's body, as if the cocoon did not contain a larva but a full-grown butterfly; however, a butterfly incapable of flying.

As a consequence, in March 1912, Mama announced to Marcello and me that we would take a nice little trip.

Why she decided to take me with her is something I still puzzle over . . . The fact remains that that morning I climbed up on the gig waiting at the door to take us from Rue Récamier to the Gare de l'Est.

I didn't understand the reason for that unexpected journey. I only knew that Marcello had to be seen by a famous Austrian doctor who would certainly find a cure for his headaches, and it was with that rationale that my brother was persuaded to undertake the journey.

My father accompanied us to the station and I remember clearly that when we entered our compartment he took mother aside for a long time. When they didn't want us to understand, Mama and Daddy spoke a funny mixture of Triestine and Ladin dialect, and I amused myself by trying to snatch a comprehensible word out of the lot: *"No desmentegà che el xé un putelo"* . . . Don't forget he's still a child.

❖

I have no memory of that train trip, probably because there was nothing to remember. Our arrival in Vienna, on the other hand, impressed me. That city reminded me somewhat of Trieste, with its wide streets, its middle-European buildings, and I was happy to find my native language — with a different inflection, however, not as singsong and less harmonious than the sweet Triestine-Austrian.

We were guests of Mama's friends (or were they relatives?) whom Marcello didn't like at all because of their old-fashioned ways. The house rules were very rigid and we were not accustomed to so much discipline. It is obvious that Marcello had imagined our stay in Vienna differently, and certainly had not considered the fact that Mama would use it to see a little of the *beau monde*. Afternoons we took walks with the nanny in the Saint Stephen quarter, or along the banks of the Danube, while Mama went with one of her innumerable girlfriends to shop for all those things "that can only be found in Vienna!"

The upshot was that, no matter if Vienna or Paris, our life was the same, with the usual *nounous*, and the only important difference that there were no tutors.

On one of those afternoons we came back a little earlier from our very boring walk because of the cold — a cold so pungent we ran to our room without taking off our overcoats. There was a pile of little colorful packages on a table marked MARCELLO in Mama's handwriting. While my brother eyed those packages curiously, I rummaged everywhere, hoping in vain to find some little gift for me too.

"Open them!" I said in disappointment, with the ill-concealed desire that they might contain some unimaginable horror.

In the meanwhile Marcello had placed the gifts in a row according to their size and color, moving deliberately at a snail's pace in order to enjoy my jealousy to the fullest.

In the first one he finally opened there was a marvelous group of Napoleon's hussars on horseback. (At least that's what Marcello said, because I was no expert and I must say that even with Marcello's know-it-all pronouncements I have some doubt, as he never played with soldiers.) Lead soldiers — each one different, each more beautiful than the other.

"What beautiful horses!"

"Don't touch them. You're too little!" he said, snatching a standard-bearer out of my hand. He was very excited, perhaps more for Mama's thinking of him than for the objects themselves. He gave me orders, for once thrilled like a normal boy his age: "Put that one there . . . This one here . . . No, stupid, don't you see they're enemies! Give it to me. You don't understand anything . . ." Then something happened. He looked in the mirror in front of him, and for some incomprehensible reason his expression changed completely. He left his soldiers where they were, and suddenly with a disgusted look he said: "If you like them so much, you play with them. I'm too big for these stupid things." In the hall I heard quick footsteps move away. That's Mama going to visit the Blumens, I thought.

One afternoon two or three days later, we put on our best clothes to go see the doctor.

Marcello, who perhaps guessed that this visit was a little out of the ordinary, was more glum than usual, and I also felt a certain tension in the air.

The building on Berggasse 19, where Dr. Freud had his office, was painted in typical pastel colors, such as are found in Czechoslovakia or Saint Petersburg. In my child's eyes it seemed like a large bluish meringue with whipped cream decoration. After the secretary led us to the waiting room, the doctor came in to introduce himself and I was charmed at once. Many times since I've been asked to describe this meeting: "What was he like?" "What did he say?" I only remember that he was very handsome, with a well-trimmed gray beard, tall, distinct, fascinating, and that I thought he was kind because he offered me some *caramels mous*.

The doctor shut himself in his office with my brother after asking Mama and me not to return before a certain hour. Mama looked put out and I believe she even protested. She said she was afraid to leave "poor Marcello" with a stranger, but what she really feared was that my brother, finding himself alone with that unusual doctor, might say or do something weird. The doctor had calm and genteel ways, but nevertheless a kind of natural authority emanated from his person that persuaded my mother to accept his request.

When we returned to his office we were left for another half hour in the waiting room without anyone coming to say anything to us. Gemma was very tense, with the anxious and uncertain air of someone who doesn't understand what she is up against, but has the strong feeling that something terrible is about to happen. And so it was, I believe, to judge by the expression on her face when we left Dr. Freud's office after a brief conversation.

Mama never wanted to tell me exactly what the diagnosis was. Even years afterward she kept her secret, letting it escape only in a few words that seem obvious today, but at the time seemed enigmatic and meaningless.

The return to Paris was very sad, as if the big hopes we had all placed in that trip had suddenly vanished. The doctor had given Marcello's illness a name, but had offered no remedy. Marcello didn't want to tell me much about his conversation, in spite of the genuine third degree I put him through. Freud had had him draw, asked him a lot of questions about us, asked him — and this made me laugh — to recount his dreams. In other words, all very odd things for a doctor to do.

"Didn't he take your temperature? Didn't he give you a physical checkup?" Marcello shook his head, obviously less interested than I in the unorthodox methods of that eccentric individual.

Everything is jumbled in my mind after that, up to the beginning of the war, which hardly touched us since my father, a fervent Irredentist, kept prudently far from Trieste. As a citizen of the Austro-Hungarian Empire, Father found himself, as did many of our compatriots, in the absurd situation of having to be in allegiance with an army destined to fight against what he considered to be his real country. For my father there were no second thoughts. We went back to Trieste for a short time, just long enough for us to organize our emigration, and we did it in such a way as to leave the city before war was declared. We were thus accepted as refugees by the Italian state, which didn't consider it necessary for my father to become part of the army of the Savoy. At the beginning of the conflict our family never stayed more than three months in one place, moving continually from one relative to another, from one community to another, where my father ushered us, almost as though he were taking advantage of the war to keep Mama from forming ties with people she met, and to prevent the inevitable troops of new admirers from swarming around her. That was when they decided to send me to a boarding school in Florence to continue my education.

"Don't go," Marcello kept repeating.

"But how can anyone study in this situation?"

"You don't have to go away to study, we'll read the textbooks together. We'll get help from a tutor, like we've always done."

The prospect of our separation was an unbearable tragedy for Marcello. Titti was still with him, of course, but their relationship was different, based essentially on the blind admiration of a little brother for an older one. With me, Marcello felt on equal ground. We had grown up together, and in spite of our differences, the awareness of there being two of us always made us feel stronger. What hurt him the most, however, was my obvious impatience: the boarding school offered me the unexpected opportunity of getting away from the asphyxiating home atmosphere, and I think Marcello viewed my anxiety to get away as a betrayal.

Some months after I left for Florence, the family was ensconced in a grand hotel in Genoa. Marcello got into the habit of writing me from there. In the beginning, one letter a day, then gradually fewer. At first he included four or five photographs in the letters: the continuation of our "photo stories," one of the many enterprises my absence had jeopardized . . . Since I was no longer there, Marcello had enlisted Titti, as well as my friend Nelly. Sometimes Mama appeared in the photos and, to tell the truth, she seemed very pleased to take part in the dramas. Among the many photographs he sent me during that time, my favorite is the one in which Marcello — in evening suit and wide silk tie, one hand leaning against the wall and the other on his brow — looks into the void with a pained expression, while Mama, guilty of some unknown misdeed, rolls her eyes pleading for pity. Nelly is not in this one, but to make up for it, Titti is seen crouched in a corner with a hand over his mouth to keep from laughing. Even today that photo makes me happy. Perhaps it is the only image of my family that conveys a vague sense of harmony to me.

I'm afraid I've lost all Marcello's letters and I'm sorry, even though the last ones were so sad and incoherent that it hurts me just to think about them. I remember, however, some sentences, and in them Marcello never spoke of himself or Titti or Mama or asked about me. They were soliloquies without beginning or end, often angry, at times almost poetic. Entire paragraphs were directly influenced by his reading, the style often bombastic and exalted. They were not at all nice, merely agonizing. A succession of meaningless monologues in which fleeting flashes of truth would emerge once in a while, too private to be understood.

Barely three weeks after the summer holiday, my father sent me a cablegram saying that in fifteen days I would have to come back to live at home. No one considered it necessary to give me an explanation for that sudden decision, but I guessed that Gemma surely had a hand in it. The family had moved again, to a villa this time, and Mama needed someone to keep an eye on Marcello so she could go about her usual life unimpeded.

As soon as I stepped in that house I realized how everything had fallen apart in just over a year.

Encouraged by Father's inexplicable absences, Gemma now

exercised her seduction with every look, every laugh, and every little gesture. She couldn't help it, and it is hard to imagine that she did it without malice, as some people claimed in her defense. It is very true that she sometimes gave the impression of not knowing how to express herself in any other way: in order to feel alive she needed to feel liked, and to be liked she was ready to fall into whatever plan was proposed to her. And thus she continued to sow more pain in Marcello's already fragile mind, as though her uncontrollable need to be loved was stronger than every possible and predictable consequence.

Therefore, to be back with Marcello was not the great joy I had imagined. Not one question about my life in Florence, not one word about the last books read, the war, the death of many of our acquaintances and friends. My presence was not enough for him anymore, or, to put it another way, my absence had given him permission to detach himself from me also, finally giving him the opportunity to slip away without my being able to do anything to stop him.

Something was different about him physically also. Something imperceptible and yet so fundamental as to almost completely transform him. I searched every detail of his face. His appearance was the same as always: he hadn't lost weight, his haircut was identical, and his mouth had the same lethargic expression.

They say the only thing that never changes about a person is the eyes. But that was exactly what was different about Marcello. Not his expression, but his eyes themselves, as if they had changed color or shape.

For some time Marcello's headaches had become so tormenting that the doctors decided to give him morphine. At the height of the war morphine was practically impossible to find and I remember taking part in the frantic search for those little phials in the terrible makeshift hospitals the Red Cross had set up here and there. That was when I discovered the war in all its horror. Because, as strange as it might seem, a family like ours in those times could continue living as if nothing was going on, ignoring the suffering of hundreds of thousands human beings. For us the war was only a conversational topic. The minds of participants at elegant dinners would be ignited with patriotic fervor, and yet those same people avoided conscription in order to be able to continue, shamelessly, their life as usual.

I was seventeen years old and my ingenuousness — or should I say my lack of awareness — could in some way justify that obtuse myopia. But what excuse did the others have?

Roaming around the hospitals I saw all those mangled, suffering boys, Marcello's contemporaries or younger, and I thanked heaven for letting us be born Austrians, and at the same time I cursed it for allowing such horrors. While I thought these things, my brother's torment became so unbearable to me that I did anything I could to get more phials, offering false excuses, even stealing . . .

How can I describe the sense of helplessness, the rage, and the pressure to act, to do something, that one feels at seeing a beloved person suffer physically? Marcello was strong, and although he had lived with the pain for years, he had now passed that limit of endurance beyond which one simply cannot go. No, for Marcello there was no longer hope for a life — I wouldn't say a happy life (an adjective completely out of place for someone like him) but at least a bearable one. Even if . . . who knows . . . perhaps Marcello could have survived that agony if the physical pain had not been accompanied by a morbid, obsessive, and excruciating love for his mother, and if Father — resigned, weak, pathetically cowardly because too, too good — had not unexpectedly given up before his son.

The morphine, obviously, wasn't limited to alleviating his pain, but little by little it penetrated Marcello's fragile body, entering his veins, enslaving him. What more suitable drug for a boy whose only objective was to escape the reality of this world, what greater folly on the doctors' part for having thought of such a remedy for someone like him? And how to forget that I, in my unforgivable ignorance, participated in that process of self-destruction?

Marcello became a morphine addict in the span of a few weeks. Morphine is like that, unforgiving, especially in the massive doses that were prescribed. Morphine alleviates pain, it helps one not to think, how could Marcello have stopped, how could he have been expected to?

When I noticed the phials were disappearing too quickly from the cabinet, I thought at first that some servant was stealing them to resell on the black market. I questioned them one by one, without saying a word to Mama in order not to exacerbate a situation that had clearly gotten out of hand. Naturally they all denied it, but a subtle irony in their replies made me suspicious. I began to watch Marcello more closely, without a precise idea, however, of what I thought I might discover. I was already aware that Marcello behaved differently in my presence, but now it seemed he wanted to avoid me — as though I were a threat, almost as though he saw in me the only person capable of understanding what was going on inside him.

When I first noticed that black case I didn't think anything of it. It seemed something for holding a pen and Marcello had many of them scattered around his room. The fact that it was hidden behind a volume of Shakespeare surprised me a little, but I attributed it to my brother's proverbial disorderliness. Some days later, while I was looking for a book in Marcello's room, I got the idea of rereading one of my favorite sonnets, which begins, "Music to hear, why hear'st thou music sadly?" As I took the book, my gaze fell again on the case. I would be lying if I said that I had a premonition; I opened it out of pure curiosity: the flash of a needle, an image barely registered on my consciousness, then the spark that triggered second thoughts, a mechanical gesture, the case falling and the syringe lying before me in all its squalor. I never said anything to anyone, not even to him. I knew that the truth

would come out in any event. I only hoped it would not be me
who had to reveal it.

Mama reacted with her usual inconsistency. On the one hand she
was ashamed of having a drug-dependent son, on the other she
was anxious about losing him permanently. And then she came
up with the solution, ready to make up for the distressing problem
she herself had caused in order to appear, in strangers' eyes, like a
Mother Courage who has tried everything and won't give up.

Even before the war ended, Marcello began a long series of hos-
pitalizations in various "sanatoriums" actually intended for the
numerous morphine and opium addicts of high society. Everyone
knew that many of these places, ostensibly responsible for curing
tuberculosis and other similar diseases, were nothing more than
detoxifying clinics.

I can just hear Gemma cleverly convincing Father of the wor-
thiness of her sacrifice, skillfully pretending to be resigned to
taking her little-loved son to those desolate deluxe hospitals, full
of upper-middle-class draft dodgers and opium addicts. I can
imagine the lies she went around telling to hide the terrible truth
that everyone knew anyway.

There's no denying that the so-called sanatoriums constituted,
during that extremely decadent time characterizing the end of an
epoch, a kind of limbo in which a certain level of society thought
it could go on for a while with the life it enjoyed in former times.
The splendid hotels, balls, social evenings transformed the sanatoriums into extremely attractive places for that disintegrating little
universe that tried, through its final and pathetic gasps, to resist
the modern world.

It was in one of those hospitals that Gemma met Castaldi, a rich
lawyer from Ferrara with ties to some friends of my father's family,
who had landed up at Villa Banunziana for opium detoxification,
although ostensibly afflicted with pleurisy. To Gemma, Castaldi
was the prototype of a fascinating man: small, stocky, receding

hairline, monocle, much younger than she, always proudly erect, with the manner of a great seducer. Mama could not help being impressed by his sure, protective, virile ways. He was the complete opposite of her husband, poor Sandrin, so mild as to seem weak, so pathetically in love as to be a nuisance. Marcello, I can imagine, observed all this with penetrating eyes, his brow nearly always frowning, and had most certainly made up his mind he would not survive this one. He had already come to that conclusion, I'm sure of it, but someone very close to him beat him to it, and he was forced to postpone his plan for a while . . .

Right after our return to Trieste I was "promised" to a young Bohemian whose father had made his fortune in Brazil, thanks to the coffee business; an arranged engagement that would allow the family, devastated by the war, by Mama's foolish expenses, and by the money wasted on Marcello, to get back on its feet. I was only eighteen years old and I was determined to find a way to get out of it, but out of respect for my father, who seemed distressed and worried, I waited patiently for the right moment to express my decision to rebel.

Marcello returned to Trieste with Mama in January 1919.
    It is impossible to find the right words to express our dismay at his physical change. It seemed like some animal was slowly stripping his flesh, sucking out every little bit of life left in him. It was almost embarrassing to look at his increasingly dazed expression, his more and more emaciated appearance, with his frequent and unexpected loss of equilibrium, nausea, spasms of uncontrollable vomiting. Even Titti was visibly distressed, as though that big brother, who loved to read him Grimm's tales in German to put him to sleep, suddenly frightened him. Not surprisingly, the only one who didn't seem to take notice was my mother: transported by the euphoria of her new love, she was oblivious to everything else, and that instinctive maternal residue that had urged her in a moment of courage — or of panic? — to undertake what she called her "great sacrifice" was by now a distant memory.

As soon as Marcello learned of my engagement he became furious with Father. It was a terrible scene, perhaps the first where he freely let himself go, as if the idea that I, his little sister, should pay the price of Mama's irresponsibility was unbearable to him; as if, after Gemma had made him witness and accomplice to her betrayal, it was impossible for Marcello to become accomplice to the ruin of my life also. In his warped mind, my father had become the person completely responsible for all the misfortunes — he who out of weakness or to preserve a peaceful life had allowed his wife to brazenly betray him; he who wanted to "sell" his daughter to compensate for his inability to curb the caprices of a woman who had long lost respect for him.

That same evening Marcello came to my room. The appallingly old-looking twenty-one-year-old man needed to look me in the face to understand if I had capitulated also, or if my resignation hid something that had escaped him. I was sitting at my desk, concentrating on writing my daily correspondence. Marcello came up to me slowly, and all at once I heard that gasping sound he had been making for several months, brought on by morphine abuse that gave him the feeling he was suffocating. I didn't feel like explaining the reason for my apparent submission to our father's absurd plan. I didn't even want to turn to look at him, because I knew I would only see disappointment. Marcello often said proudly that I was the strongest, the one who could always be gently assertive. This time I hadn't even tried, and he found that incomprehensible.

I finally turned his way, avoiding his gaze. Marcello merely stared at me in amazement, taking in my every facial movement, every blink of my eye, as though he needed nothing more in order to understand. He backed up, sat on the bed, and murmured softy, sweetly: "Now, explain it to me . . . I am so tired . . ."

After that day, Marcello stayed by my side and supported me in my waiting strategy. I had somehow been able to convince him that I had chosen the only possible way out: to pretend to agree in order to build the basis for a refusal. We both knew our weak father too well not to know that, by making the right moves, we could manipulate him. All we had to do was give him the impression that everything was always and in every way the product of his own will. That was how my mother was often able to make him accept the worst humiliations, and that was the way, for this once, I decided to act to save my future.

Life in Trieste in those times was very exciting. The city had returned to being Italian again, and my family happily cast off its Austrian citizenship. It became practically impossible to express oneself in German in salons, and at every dinner party the future opening before us was passionately discussed. The exaltation, hope, euphoria were also tied to the reconstruction: a period in which businesses would be able to thrive and prosper.

Apparently my father's work remained impervious to those positive effects, or perhaps his situation was already too compromised to draw any advantage from them. We'll never know, as he disappeared, taking his secret with him.

Marcello posed as a decadent dandy. More intolerant than ever of the four walls of the house that we were forced to rent after ours was sequestered, he affected total indifference to our father's business affairs, almost as if they didn't concern him at all.

The only person who could give his tormented soul a little relief was Titti. That little tyke had always worked a sort of magic on us, and we would often look at him in amazement, as though discovering a flower in the middle of a desert. After Marcello returned home he discovered the pleasure of getting involved in the education of his little nine-year-old brother, already so mature and happy to be in the world. They spent many hours in Titti's room, or they went on secret walks through who knows what city streets. The complicity that grew between them slowly and inevitably excluded me from Marcello's life. But I was not hurt by it. In fact, I put much hope in this new relationship, because I perceived in his interest in Titti an *élan vital* that had been too lacking in his life of late. However, it was necessary to stay alert

and make sure that that closeness didn't become a danger for the
still so small and defenseless little boy.

In the meanwhile Mama's relationship with Castaldi had become
public knowledge, so that my father almost quit pretending to be
in the dark. It seemed like nothing bothered him, and in reality
that's the way it was, since by now he had undoubtedly decided
what to do.

Marcello had also decided what he would do, but in his own
way and style.

The stifling smell of opium or morphine took over his room,
and his nearly constant delirium rarely allowed him to be with us.

After the war we remained in Trieste a little less than a year. Time
enough for Father to get things in order, to recuperate the little
that had not been sequestered, to choose Italian citizenship, and
to leave for Genoa, where the Villa delle Rose awaited us — the
last foolish thing my father did for Gemma.

Surprisingly, there were a large number of Irredentists who
had also chosen to live in Genoa, making it easy for Gemma to
transfer her Triestine habits there. She organized dinner-debates
in which everyone showed off his political know-how and
designed Italy's future. At Villa delle Rose these meetings or dinners took place almost every Monday and both Marcello and I
were obliged to participate.

Frankly, I never understood why Gemma was so keen on
having us present, considering the embarrassment Marcello was
likely to cause — not only for his obviously poor physical condition, but also because his every comment assumed a provocative
tone. The habitués paid no attention to his eccentricities, but the
new arrivals seemed dismayed by his startling remarks.

To accentuate the discomfort, Marcello enjoyed speaking in
German or nostalgically evoking the grandeur of the Empire,
slinging sarcasm at anyone who challenged him, and especially
Gemma, who till then never cared about nationalism and who
would suddenly exhibit zealous patriotism.

With remarkable self-destruction, my father took to inviting to those dinners my fiancé, who was afraid of appearing discourteous to the family by refusing. The evenings with him were truly an ordeal, because in his presence Marcello's pro-Austrian ranting was even more relentless and ridiculous. As much as I tried to protect him from the intellectual humiliation he exposed himself to, his total loss of self-esteem gave my brother a strange pleasure in appearing completely incoherent, a luxury his pride had not allowed him up to that time.

It was one of those evenings that my father chose for his tragic performance. This time, however, he outdid himself, since besides my poor Brazilian fiancé and his parents, he had also succeeded in getting Castaldi to come.

When we sat down to eat, only Marcello was missing, and Father asked me to go find him.

I knocked softly on his door and entered.

My brother was lying on a Persian rug scattered with Oriental pillows. He was smoking a hookah, eyes on the ceiling, while I stared at him in annoyance.

Suddenly he left the water pipe on the floor and sat on his bed, with a defiant look:

"It's no use. I'm not going."

"Oh, yes you are, because you've got to help me."

"I can't help you."

"Not if you desert me."

I cannot remember anything more embarrassing than that ridiculous dinner where everyone looked at one another knowing and pretending not to know, hiding the truth behind trite phrases and double meanings pathetically clear to everyone; a terrible masquerade forced upon us by our father, almost as if it were his first and last victory.

It happened before dessert, or maybe after, I don't know. Father got up, excusing himself with the diners, and left the room. Barely four or five minutes passed before the explosion, an eternity before we were able to open that wretched door . . .

Marcello was dumbfounded, stunned — not exactly by grief, but rather by a sense of betrayal. How could he? He beat him to it! The weak one, the docile one, had acted first, without bothering to send those clear signals that Marcello had been launching so theatrically over the years, almost creating a sense of immunity in those around him . . .

It took Marcello about two years to find the strength to follow him, two years that gave a definite turn to my fate, making me feel I was its one and only master.

Right after my father's death I broke my ridiculous engagement without worrying about form or consequence, and decided to find a job. I wanted to break every family tie, and although I tried to hide it from myself, I soon realized my decision included Marcello also. I cannot explain why, but I felt an awful resentment toward him . . . I was angry with him for forcing me to concentrate on his suffering, making me less concerned about the one who was obviously even more fragile. I could not forgive him for having monopolized my attention, for having always been at the center of my worries. I blamed him in order not to blame myself.

Mama let the customary year pass before marrying Castaldi, and Marcello . . . Marcello was by then far away, somewhere else, in the final limbo of his earthly existence, no longer angry, no longer jealous, but prostrate, immobile, still, like a run-down phonograph. He searched in vain, many times, for the courage his father had and in the end he succeeded — I'm convinced of it — almost in spite of himself, by chance. He was found in his car near a beach at Marina di Pisa on the night of August 24, 1923, already rigid, with foam on his mouth, a syringe clenched in his hand, and his veins full of morphine.

GEMMA

I'VE NEVER had a good memory. I always need the reminder of photographs and diaries, as if my memory couldn't function without props.

And anyway, it's not easy to talk about Marcello. Because Marcello had not one, but many, a thousand different faces, a thousand souls that were never at peace.

Without a doubt he was born too soon, because in 1898, how old was I? Nineteen? And anyway, it seemed like he was born without advance warning, like a little creature that pops up suddenly, a jack-in-the-box.

Thinking back over his birth, the delivery, I ask myself if it's really possible that I don't remember a thing about my firstborn coming into the world?

The pain, the fatigue, the yelling . . . yes, I remember that. The little blows from his clenched fists that were so strong he kept hurting himself, and the wet nurse who cut his fingernails regularly . . .

Let's face it: I wasn't very capable. I didn't know how to hold or caress him, and so I let the nanny do it, or Sandrin who always had more patience.

The truth is I never imagined becoming a mother so soon.

On the other hand, I remember his circumcision very well. It was impossible to get out of, even though it seemed like a savage ritual to me. The mohel had beautiful long hands — an old man's hands, I thought, hands that inspire confidence. I heard Marcello cry and said to myself: "Those hands can't do him harm."

He was so odd, with wisps of black hair covering his little eyes. He already had a grown-up's serious, dark, deep expression.

Everyone insisted on putting him in my arms, and I would raise a fuss: "You'll see I'll break his bones!" I was so afraid I might drop him. And I may have done so once, but now I'm not sure.

I don't remember the nurse's name. Without a doubt there were many.

One must have been Hungarian, because Marcello hummed an aggravating Gypsy lullaby for a long time. I tried to make him forget it by teaching him a little song in Ladin that my mama sang to me, except that I couldn't remember the words and had to invent them, making a big *mismas*.

That's all. Nothing else comes to mind.

There was a sort of void that lasted until Dolores came along, Dolores called Dolly.

Poor child. How could I have given her such a sad name? And yet I'm the one who chose it, I'm sure of that.

It must have been the heroine of some novel I liked, who knows . . .

Anyway, there I was. At twenty I had two babies.

Two babies born in a year and a half.

Certainly I was a little discombobulated. Who wouldn't have been?

I hadn't expected that when I got married. I thought I would enjoy life a little. I did everything I could not to end up like my sister Eugenia, who married a rabbi; instead I was almost worse off than she.

I had barely left home, full of desires and curiosity, and not in the least inclined to be caged up again.

Anyway, Sandrin understood this.

One of the few who did, you know! Because the others were always great at watching and criticizing: "Gemma's always in motion. She never sees her children. She's always showing off."

Sandrin understood, because he enjoyed my enthusiasm, my high spirits, my desire to be always on the go.

He wasn't one of those who wanted to curb me, mold me, or shut me up in a little box. Not yet . . .

Marcello and Dolly were my little pets. I liked to see them all decked out for a walk with the nanny, dressed alike, perfect. I liked knowing they were there, but I was not very experienced as a mother, not with them, because I didn't know how to be yet.

How can you bring up children when you've barely had time to grow up yourself?

Old Giulio was convinced that by sending us to Egypt he would be doing me a great disservice. Poor man. He didn't understand anything about his daughter-in-law. He was sure I would be terrorized by the idea of ending up in such a faraway land, a country of savages. He thought this was a way of punishing me for going around Trieste with "the belly showing." As he continually reminded everyone: "You'll see how this will settle Gemma down."

Sandro and I often laughed about his surprise at my enthusiastic reception of the news.

"Papa still doesn't understand that Gemma isn't afraid of anything," Sandro would say proudly to his friends, and with equal pride I was already thinking about the wardrobe I would have to get together in order to be at the top of the game.

For dates, details, clear memories, I'm certainly not the right person. That is Dolly's department. My life is an assortment of impressions. And those of Egypt are some of the best. Not only for the colors, the colonial setting, the elegance, and strangeness of the circumstance, but because it was simply the ideal place for a woman like me.

Marcello would have been about three or four years old in Cairo. He was still the right age for games. And Marcello was very particular about what game. He had no patience for balls or hoops. The only thing he really liked to do was to run like a demon through the dusty park without paying me the slightest heed. He also had a mania for hiding in the ironing room, among the steam irons and bare feet of the girls who would laugh like crazy when they saw him on all fours among the presses. He was wild, undisciplined, a small and thin little fellow. Beautiful he was not. He had never been. But he had a sad, dark look that touched your heart. Even when he laughed (because he did laugh when he was little), his eyes seemed something separate from the rest of his face, different, as if they were on their own. Sometimes it amused me to watch him from a distance. If out of affection, I don't know; delight, I don't believe so . . . let's say I was curious.

The children were happy in Cairo, like two unfettered puppies, because it was impossible to keep after them in that *mismas*. Sandrin and I had little time and the nannies, well, let's not go into that!

But they were as happy as could be, so free . . .

When I think about Egypt one word comes to mind more than any other: *freedom.* We all felt free: the children because they were too young to be burdened by studies, Sandro because he had full responsibility for the Cairo branch, me because I could project the image that best represented me at that particular time. I could be what I was and not what I was expected to be, without fear of criticism.

Marcello was a little weird, it's true, but aren't all children at that age? He always ran around in the garden, his nose in the air like a hunting dog, and hid in ambush for me. He enjoyed frightening me, and when he saw me jump he laughed like crazy. I laughed, too, to tell the truth, but there was already something about his excitement that made me uncomfortable. And besides that, his speech was odd. I don't believe Marcello spoke his first full sentence until he was five years old. But little did he care! He was so sure we understood him in any case. But he was wrong about that . . . because we all had trouble understanding him from the first.

"My Marcello is a bit of a scamp," I wrote Mama.

A rowdy little scamp. Period.

Once in a while I get a kick out of looking at pictures taken at the time: they are so far from the truth. Marcello always seems to be posing, so well dressed and proper, a real little prince . . . nothing like that boy who spun like a top. Yes, because that's what Marcello was in the Cairo days: a kid who ran around in the dust with his little nose in the air.

After two years we returned to Trieste. Too soon for my liking, but that was Giulio's decision and there was little room for argument.

Marcello went along without reacting. At sight he seemed to be the same wild boy as always, but really he was different, gloomier. His similarity to a small animal had changed; now he seemed more like a panther in ambush.

"Tell me. Are you sorry you left Cairo?" he was often asked.

"Mama likes Trieste because there's the sea," he would reply, pleased to put off his interlocutors with an answer that had nothing to do with the question.

After that exotic parenthesis, my salon was more successful than ever. Not that I did anything to deserve it; but we obviously aroused curiosity. It was Dora who asked me to take up my *jour* again, and in a very short time Sandro and I found we never had a free evening. On the rare times we had one, we went to the Teatro Grande (or was it already called the Verdi then?). We went out a lot then; those were the good times, the time of the Empire, before the catastrophe and war.

❖

I always knew the children were sitting on the stairs to watch us when we went out in the evening. It was Marcello's idea. And anyway, there was nothing wrong with it. They wanted to see the clothes, the jewels — they enjoyed themselves, in other words. I could hear them giggling like two little idiots and so I would deliberately pause at the door and turn to let them admire me. I knew I was making them happy.

Sandro decided the time had come for them to study with tutors. Serious lessons, with grades, homework, *et tout le bataclan*. Marcello was less than enthusiastic, but I didn't worry about it; he was still so young there would be lots of time for learning! Every once in a while I asked the tutor how it was going, and he would barely answer me. It was obvious he was not pleased. But as long as he didn't have a specific complaint . . .

When I went to visit the Levi grandparents I always took the children with me. I got a kick out of dressing them alike, and as they were nearly contemporaries, they looked like twins. We took the carriage and would usually alight and walk partway. I would do anything to be late, and as the little tads weren't crazy about their grandparents' company, it was easy to talk them into stopping for a hot chocolate at the Café degli Specchi, or better still, stopping a minute in the Old Town for a *mussolada*. If my mother-in-law Volumnia had seen us what a face she would have made!

Marcello got very excited when we went out together. He talked a mile a minute and couldn't stay still. On the other hand, if we happened to meet someone he got flustered, blushed, looked at his feet, and began stammering. It irked me to see him suddenly become so awkward and stupid, and I couldn't be sure it was due to timidity. Thinking back over it now, I wonder if he didn't want to make me look bad. But he was probably still too young to have such perverse ideas . . .

He started following me around the house. I teased him about it, but he didn't stop. He was always right behind me. Every once in a while he'd grab my skirt and say: "Now try to get away." I would make a joke of it and try to get free. But Marcello clung so tightly that more than once we almost fell over.

Sandrin said to ignore him. "He's still a little rapscallion," he said. "He'll grow out of it."

We followed Sandrin to Milan. I didn't like that city at all, but Sandro had several months of work there and we didn't have a choice. It is in Milan where fate played its bitterest trick: saving Marcello's life in exchange for a long agony. Thanks be to God, as my sister says.

It's true I've never been very courageous.

What can I do about it? It's not that I don't want to be, it's that a child's pain is not like the pain of others.

It's different.

So very different.

And besides, when Marcello suffered, he suffered all over. With his whole body. He perspired so much that the women had to change his sheets six times a day. He beat his head back and forth, and with such strength!

I couldn't watch him, so I had to go out.

From his room, and also from the house.

Sandrin, however, understood my weaknesses. He knew he was stronger than I and didn't blame me.

In order not to become ill myself I had to pretend nothing was going on. It happens. Not everyone is good at facing catastrophe. Sandro was there, the nurses were there; that was enough. They were much better than I would be. They had something that kept them going: a wonderful strength. The kind of strength I found years later, but not then, not there.

Marcello's condition remained the same for days, maybe weeks.

Then the fever broke and he stopped raving.

Sandrin told me that after Marcello woke up he had asked for me, but — something surprising for him — he had spoken in dialect.

This is something that still puzzles me. Why dialect, if dialect had always aggravated him so much, and if it unnerved him every time a word of dialect slipped out of my mouth?

The crisis seemed to have passed. To make him laugh I improvised fashion shows in his room — with hats, because he liked those the best. I would hide behind the screen, that green one with Chinese dragons that has always been in his room, and I would come out in a different hat every time. Marcello would close his eyes and not open them until I told him to. Then he, a real connoisseur, would comment on every model. It was nice to see that frail, weak boy sit up in bed and get so excited about such a silly game! He was carried away by it all, sometimes leaping up to straighten a brim or remove a ribbon; then he would fall back in bed and look at me with great satisfaction. I tried to keep him calm and quiet, because the doctor said not to let him get worked up, but it wasn't easy. He would go from prostration to elation, as if after that long period of delirium and sleep he needed to make up for lost time. The only thing that calmed him down a little were Triestine songs . . . That's right, there were those too, I had almost forgotten: the dialect irritated him, but he really liked those songs.

I would refuse him nothing, and I was happy because he had stopped banging his head back and forth.

Finally the doctor said we could return to Trieste, that Marcello could stand the trip. I thought it would make him happy, but instead he didn't want to hear about it. He began to shout and thrash around, even making himself ill.

"I don't want to go to Trieste. There are too many people in Trieste. I get tired."

"I don't understand? What makes you tired?"

"I get tired waiting for you come home in the evening."

"What do you mean? Why should you ever wait for me?"

❖

My memories about what happened after we went back to Trieste are a little confused. With all that coming and going the memory easily gets muddled. Of the whole succession of tutors I only remember Pierre, the Frenchman, who always complained about Marcello. I couldn't really blame him . . . Marcello was intelligent, even too much so, but I wonder what intelligence is good for if it only makes you arrogant!

Anyway, I decided not to bother with his education. In the first place, it was a man's thing, and besides Marcello made me nervous always trying to give me a hard time. He laughed at my questions; he gave wrong answers on purpose just to see if I would notice. He even started correcting me when a word of dialect escaped.

He had an obsession for Tuscan, "the pure language," he said, and every time he teased me I would respond drily: "Look, when I wish, my Tuscan is much purer than yours. And seeing that you like to rinse your mouth in the Arno so much, I don't understand why you keep refusing to go to boarding school in Florence . . ."

It was so beautiful in Trieste, you can't even imagine! Elegant, cosmopolitan, in the center of everything. And we were in the center of Trieste.

That may be why I can't say much about the children. That was a time when I was intoxicated with the whirl of meetings, parties, concerts; few images of the children have survived.

The tutors talked us into separating Dolly and her brother. I'm sure they were right, but I was sorry because those two were a little like twins, always together chattering, laughing, inventing strange games. However, I also realized that they couldn't learn anything together, and besides Marcello's headaches had started up again.

They no longer studied together, but they continued to hole up in a room all afternoon.

Oh, there's no denying it; they had imagination to burn.

I know because sometimes I could hear them talking behind the closed door. They dressed up; they acted out their favorite fairy tales, or they would pretend to be "Sandro and Gemma going to the theater," or "Gemma who receives on Thursdays."

Children's games, nothing more, except that sometimes Marcello got too wrapped up in his role. I don't know exactly how to explain it, but I was less than pleased with some of his imitations.

That Marcello loved the theater was no mystery to anyone, and he didn't limit himself to those little plays with Dolly: he was very good at acting in real life. More and more often he would pretend to have fits, and you should have seen how good he was at making himself sick! When he had homework to do, when I went out in the evening, when I left for a vacation, or when I threatened to send him to boarding school.

Sandro would always let himself get taken in, but not me. If I had planned to do something I did it anyway. Just imagine if I had let that kid dictate the rules!

From the time he was a child Marcello had always been unkempt, down in the mouth, with a manner that fluctuated between melancholy and rage. He was a little like what the Triestines called a *pìtima*: exasperating, sickly, discontented.

I never saw him play — I mean really play, and not running around like a maniac just to work off steam. I can't remember a single toy. Yet he had them, because Sandrin was always bringing home heaps of surprises for the children. I have no idea where they ended up . . .

Marcello enjoyed singing with me, toying with my hair, playing hide and seek — things like that. But I don't believe I ever saw him with a toy soldier in his hand, or a peashooter . . .

And then all those weird things: he drew very well, rapid sketches that he would tear up so no one would see them. As for his poems, he burned them, to have no doubts as to their final destruction.

In Trieste, if by chance I happened to have nothing else to do in the afternoon, I would organize a tea or bridge party. When we had guests it seemed only natural for the children to come greet them. In fact, I considered it essential.

Dolly was always well mannered and polite, while Marcello

would sulk. If anyone put out a hand to caress his head he would step back without even looking up, and if one of the guests would express the misguided wish to hear Dolly play a piece on the piano, he would pontificate that his sister was not a *chien savant*, with that lame guffaw he thought disguised his arrogance.

He always went around with his drawing pad, and every time I confiscated his charcoal he managed to get more somehow. He would hide in a corner and draw, sure of attracting someone's attention, probably mine, because he knew very well that I didn't appreciate those dreadful sketches. That was why he tore them up, swearing to me, as he looked me straight in the face, that he never made them.

Sandro begged me to be patient; hadn't the doctors said that Marcello would never be the same after his illness? Yet, there was something suspicious about the way that child hid behind his illness when it suited him. I always thought Marcello was much more aware than he wanted us to believe, and that his behavior was an expression of something that went far beyond the simple aftermath of meningitis.

His deterioration coincided with the decision to move to Paris. He didn't like the idea, that is certain, even if I don't remember why, but maybe he never said. I had my theory, because I had noticed for some time that as soon as he realized I was enthusiastic about something, he would grow sullen. He didn't want to go to Paris, just as he hadn't wanted to return to Trieste, just as he had refused to go to boarding school. "Maybe he's afraid of change," Sandro said. Yes, well, he was especially afraid of what might please me. That's the truth.

The move to Paris was very chaotic. I had a million things to do, and among these, there were also Marcello's demands to have his room in Paris exactly like the one he left in Trieste. I believe, in fact, that this was one of the many conditions Sandro accepted to make him happy. A ten-year-old boy — were we crazy? He wrapped his "objects" one by one as though they were Sèvres porcelain. Sandrin smiled about his fussiness. "After all it's a healthy occupation."

When I found out I was pregnant again, the idea of having to tell the children made me extremely anxious. I don't know why . . . it was Marcello I was afraid of. I felt he might react badly and I was tired of his weird ways. Instead, after a moment of uncertainty, he must have decided that the news could be to his advantage; it could provide a good pretext for keeping me under his control. "I read an article that said that a woman in an interesting state should sleep a lot and avoid long periods of sitting." . . . "Do you know that jolts in a carriage are bad for the baby?" . . . "Be careful when going in public places because you might catch some disease."

He behaved like a husband — actually worse, because Sandrin would never have made such comments. Then, when my belly started to swell, he began to look at me in a strange way, with all kinds of mad contortions to avoid seeing that irritating protuberance. He talked about the baby like it was a ballast, a chain that had to keep me housebound; otherwise he pretended not to notice, forcing himself to forget that soon someone would come out from there.

We spent the summer in Menton. I was the one who suggested we go there, because even in that condition I couldn't do without the sea. Actually it was foolish: I was so tired, so big and ugly, that I soon had to give up the idea of swimming.

At first I went to the beach anyway, but what sense was it if I couldn't wear a bathing costume? I was so put out that in the end I decided not even to go sit on the beach. What was the point if I couldn't go in the water? And besides, I felt ridiculous being there in my street clothes like an Englishwoman.

Luckily Dora and her husband had come to join us at the hotel. Sandro was annoyed when he found out: "Can't we go any-where without your Triestine court in tow?" What court? Dora was my best friend, the only one I completely trusted. And anyway it was her idea: after her last visit to Paris she had been concerned about certain problems I had shared with her, and she gave me some advice I had followed. Now she wanted to verify with her own eyes the success of her plan:

"You're really beautiful."

"Oh, hardly. I'm round as a ball. Some idea you had."

"You'll see, it will work."

"Maybe with Sandro. But with Marcello . . ."

"What does Marcello have to do with it now?"

Indeed, he had something to do with it. The hotel wasn't full because it was early — June, I think — and still a little too chilly for swimming. I've always liked June just for that reason, because I can't stand hot weather. Besides the Pristers and us there were three or four families, all with children much younger than ours. Dolly loved to swim and was good at it. I don't believe I ever saw Marcello even try. It's true that it could be very dangerous if he had one of his fits in the water. But once again I had the impression that he didn't want to learn to swim only because it would have pleased me so much. Every day Dolly made a wide sweep with Attilio, whom I trusted blindly. One morning while she was still rather far from the shore, she got a cramp: if I had to count all the times that has happened to me! As soon as her brother realized the situation he seemed to lose all control. He started screaming like a maniac at Attilio, who was accompanying his sister to the shore, accusing him of wanting to kill her. Dolly tried to calm him, but there was no way, and Marcello worked himself up to such a state he had a fit. Cesarina came running to me as I was peacefully drinking tea with Dora. Poor thing! Dora jumped up at once, and I shuffled along behind her with my big belly. By the time I got to the beach Dora was already there trying to calm him: now Mama's here, she said, everything is all right, nothing happened . . . The convulsions were over and Marcello had calmed down, but he hadn't opened his eyes. He remained still for a while without saying a word. Then, with eyes still closed, he snarled: "It's her fault she took it into her head to swim, and if she had died it would be nobody's fault but hers."

Dora brought me a Delphos dress from Venice. It had been her idea, because imagine if I could still keep up with Fortuny's creations in Paris! When I took it out of the box I was so surprised that I wanted to try it on at once. It just had to fit, I had to show it to Sandrin! Goodness, how beautiful those pleats were over my round belly, how nicely they fell. It seemed made to measure for me, and Dora had chosen such a warm, elegant plum color . . . Going down the stairs to join our husbands, we laughed like two schoolgirls playing a trick on their parents. We ran down the stairs, and I remember Dora cautioning: "Take it easy, in your state. Watch out!" But I ignored her and kept going, impatient, excited, sure of my effect . . . Then a door opened and I saw Marcello slip out, followed by the nanny whom I believe wanted to stop him. He had most certainly heard us laughing and had hurried out to see what was going on. I had no intention of stopping. It was Dora who paused to speak to him. Marcello made no sign of having seen her, concentrated as he was on fixing me with his look of exasperation: "Does Papa know you are going around the hotel in your nightgown?"

He stood there like an offended fiancé, full of insufferable arrogance: how can he think of judging me, that infant . . . and instinctively I wanted to slap him. I raised my hand, but at the last minute I stopped myself, just a finger from his face. I gripped his chin, and with an enormous effort of self-control, I hissed: "Now you go back to your room and if you ever dare talk to me like that again, you will regret it." That is what I said, and not a word more. Dora stood there like stone, perhaps more surprised by my behavior than by Marcello's. He turned white, began to gasp for breath and hold his head in his hands, with that pleading look he had learned to use when he no longer felt in control of the situation. Then I heard myself saying to the nurse: "Call a doctor because I have no time to lose with his dramas," and I turned on my heels, leaving him there, panting, alone with his cheap blackmail.

Dora followed me down the stairs, upset: "Gemma, how can

you be so hard on the little fellow? Didn't you see he was ill?"
Certainly I saw it. I see it over and over. I began to explain that
every time that boy saw I was happy, excited about something, he
tried to ruin everything . . . I've never seen such a thing, Dora
said. The child doesn't exist who does that. Well, you've certainly
seen it now. Just ask Sandrin about it, if he has the guts to give you
a straight answer.

Sandro and Attilio were playing cards on the terrace. When they
saw us coming we must certainly have looked very upset. Sandro
briefly commented on the Delphos dress, but then stopped
almost at once. He realized something had happened and had
probably also guessed with whom. He had the embarrassed look
on his face of someone who hopes the subject will change. But
Dora — never famous for her diplomatic tact — had already
begun telling all about it in her usual excited way:
    "Excuse me for saying so, but it seems to me that there is
something wrong with that boy."
    "In case you've forgotten, he had a serious case of meningitis
when he was nine years old."
    At that point Attilio put in his two cents: "Pardon me, Sandro,
but meningitis has little to do with it. I don't want to seem to be
meddling, I know it's your problem, but . . ."
    Sandro was furious, but I was the only one who noticed. He
pretended to concentrate on his cards; he stroked his mustache
nervously but kept quiet. We remained like that for a short time,
waiting uneasily for someone to conclude, to add something . . .
Then, suddenly, Attilio began to talk about that doctor, that odd
man I had already heard about. He told about his methods, saying
they talked of nothing else in Trieste, especially in the community, and "not only because he is Jewish, but also because he
seems to have made some really surprising discoveries; he man-
ages to get into people's minds . . ."
    "Come on . . ."
    "Yes, Sandro, that's right. He can get into people's minds and
cure nervous diseases."

In those times Freud was almost unknown, and I must say I didn't know a great deal about him. Actually in Trieste they had talked for some time about Weininger, someone I didn't like at all because of all his remarks against the community and women. Attilio maintained that even Edoardo Weiss, whom I knew well because I had often seen him at the home of my Morpurgo relatives, had gone to Vienna to attend Freud's lectures. All things considered, it might be interesting at least to look into, "if only for curiosity's sake." Oh, Lord! He had used the wrong argument, because if there was anything Sandrin did not understand, it was curiosity. New things made him suspicious. Just like my grandfather who always said, "Never leave the old road for the new."

We didn't mention it again throughout dinner. Only when we went to bed that evening did I say something like, "Know what I think I'll do? Tomorrow I'll write a letter to that doctor to see what he says." Sandrin didn't even take the trouble to answer me, but his look was enough to let me know that I wouldn't do a blessed thing the next day.

And in fact, I didn't send that letter until much later, from the Paris apartment, the one on Rue Récamier, where Giorgio — Titti — was born, my golden-headed little boy, my love, my Nacci.

That delivery, yes, I do remember that one. Because with Titti everything was different right from his birth: painless, serene, quick. And he was already so beautiful . . .

I became an anxious mother: I didn't like having to leave him with the nurse, and I didn't even like for Sandro to pick him up. Not to mention Dolly!

Marcello didn't try to, but you could see he loved him. He wasn't jealous; he always looked at him tenderly. He would tell him stories, sing him songs. For months a great calm reigned in the house, a great harmony. Our little angel pacifier had arrived, as Sandro put it.

Then, I don't know how, everything started all over again.

Perhaps because I began going out some in the evenings, staying home less. The fact is that Marcello returned to the attack . . . His tactics changed. Now he chastised me (and in such a way!) for not taking care of Titti as I should.

But I kept my secret weapon in reserve and knew that the more Marcello acted up the easier it would be to coerce Sandro into accepting my plan.

It's hard to explain such an awful situation to someone who hasn't experienced it. Boiling down that feeling of desperation to simple facts or words seems practically impossible. A thin line divided us from him. Marcello went from foolish chatter to total silence. A silence that could last for days, without anyone, not even Dolly, having any idea why. *Il joue à ricochets* I always said when he got that way, because his face reminded me of those sad little ponds children skipped rocks over.

Sandrin bought him a gramophone and he listened to music while sitting arms crossed on his bed. Sometimes he closed his eyes or stared out the window, but mostly he stayed passionately absorbed in one of those books too advanced for his age. He was capable of playing the same record thirty times in a row. And if anyone dared ask him to turn down the volume or change the record, he would turn out his light and stay in the dark. Because of his headache, he said. And I would answer: "*Si tu as mal à la tête, comment peux-tu supporter un tel boucan?*"

I don't believe he ever had friends his own age. And where could he have met them? He didn't want to go on picnics, and if he should ever happen to run into some little boy he would stand there awkwardly observing him without a clue what he should do.

He only had patience with Titti.

And so, at first I thought: well then, he has found his niche; after all, if he's happy this way, what does it really matter? . . . I forgot that "once an evil makes its nest it never leaves," as my mama would say.

❖

He followed me everywhere. He had even started entering my room without knocking. Once I even slapped him — a hard one, the kind that leaves a mark.

Sandrin made light of it. He said that after an illness like that it was natural to get confused, and besides he was at a difficult age, but I shouldn't worry, it would all soon pass. I decided he was right. The headaches were what made him nervous. He behaved that way because he didn't feel well, of course . . .

That he was not well was now obvious to everyone. But it was not only the aftereffects of meningitis, and at a certain point it became difficult to keep denying the obvious. That was when I remembered Freud, the "magician of psychoanalysis," the one Attilio had spoken about. So, without asking Sandrin's permission — he would have said no right away anyway — I wrote him a letter with the help of a friend who had attended some lectures at the Salpêtrière and was somewhat familiar with his theories. Not long afterward I was given an appointment.

Who knows what Marcello was expecting from that trip; who knows what stories he got in his head . . .

He received the news of our impending trip to Vienna with exaggerated elation, and I didn't like his enthusiasm one bit. I knew where such overexcitement could lead. He told everyone that the trip had been organized for him, that we were going there to make him well, that it would be something special. Basically that was the way it was, even if he did make it sound merely like a pleasure trip.

As soon as we arrived in Vienna, Marcello realized that everything was a little different from the way he had imagined it. For starters, Dora came to meet us at the station with a car, and he hadn't expected to find her there. He didn't like the Pristers, especially Dora, even though she had always treated him kindly. Marcello only knew that she and I acted "a little crazy," as Sandrin said, and it embarrassed him. Besides, he thought we were staying in a hotel. I had to tell him: "Don't you know it's not fitting for a woman unaccompanied by her husband to stay in a hotel?"

No, he didn't know. He'd never thought about it. "Well then, why does Papa let you go to the theater and dinners alone?"

"Oh, Lord, what does that have to do with this now?"

The Weberns, the distant cousins we stayed with, were a bit old-fashioned, even though I must say that all Vienna seemed like a city frozen in time.

Marcello immediately showed his hostility toward them, and to make them understand, he started calling attention to their every little foible. He criticized their habits, their food; he broke into laughter with his sister in front of their guests. He imitated their Austrian accent, he aped the slightly *démodé* way poor Eveline had of doing things, but luckily she didn't notice anything. In other words, he decided to make himself unpleasant and succeeded to perfection.

One day, in an effort to change his mood a little, I asked Dora to take me to Schwartz, the famous store near Stefanplatz. I got the idea, Lord knows why, of buying Marcello some lead soldiers, and as everyone spoke of this Schwartz as a true artist, I was anxious to see his handiwork.

When I got back with my colored packages, I was so excited by the idea of surprising Marcello that I went straight to the children's room. But the room was empty, so I decided to leave everything there and wait for them to return from their walk.

Then the maid came with a message from the Liebermanns inviting me to join them for tea or some such and I got ready to go out. When I came back down, dressed and ready to leave with my new mink muff, I heard the children's voices and went to their room. Marcello had opened two or three packages and was standing with his back to me, carefully observing a foot soldier. He stood still for a few seconds, with that toy soldier suspended midair in front of him. Then, as though he had suddenly come to his senses, he threw the packages in the air, telling Dolly that poor Mama thought he was still a baby, that not even Titti played with toy soldiers anymore, and that

because I was always running around, I hadn't even noticed I
had a son close to his bar mitzvah.

I closed the door quietly and left.

The Weberns had a box at the Vienna Opera, one of those lovely,
spacious boxes in the center that on grand occasions became true
and proper drawing rooms. I loved going with them — not so
much for the music, because Wagner was the fashion, and those
interminable operas tired me — but for the pleasure of the
encounters, the show of dresses, the conversation. Everyone
seemed so interesting, refined, cultured, without the mania *de
jouer les modernes* that obsessed the Parisians. As soon as my
cousin said I was in Vienna to take my son to Dr. Freud, everyone
looked at me with much interest. "What courage, Signora, to
undertake such a journey for your son . . . you absolutely must
have dinner with us and tell us everything . . ." "That's the way it
always is. They have to come from Paris to make us realize we
have our own celebrities!"

Really, it didn't seem to me like I had done anything out of the
ordinary; however, I must admit that I wasn't indifferent to the
admiration I felt I aroused . . . the point is that the idea of
appearing as a woman *hors du commun* wasn't at all displeasing.

There's no denying that Freud was good looking, tall, slender,
distinguished — but not the least pleasant or affable. When I
came into his office he didn't even look at me. Not that I cared so
much, but anyway, a little glance, even out of politeness . . .
Nothing . . . He seemed to have deliberately turned his back to
watch the falling snow. I waited, at first with patient respect, then
with growing irritation. When he turned, the first thing he said to
me was: "Wasn't I supposed to see a boy?" Like that. Not a good
day or a how are you. "We can talk afterward, because it's better to
avoid outside interference before seeing him. Therefore, I'm
sorry, but it will be better for us to meet around six; in that way I'll
have something to say to you. I may not have formed a diagnosis
yet, but at least I'll have a picture of the situation . . ."

❖

I felt I was listening to an actor wearily repeating lines he had spoken a thousand times. Far from fascinating and mysterious, I thought; maybe Sandrin was right: that man had all the aspects of an imposter.

To be back at six meant wandering around town for nearly three hours. And what was I supposed to do with Dolly all that time? I thought of taking her to one of those wonderful cafés where you can read newspapers and hear poetry readings, but I wasn't sure Dolly would like it. What would an eleven-year-old girl like? Sandro often talked to the children, especially with Dolly, and I asked myself what could he ever discuss with such a shy and reticent child. For the first time I believe I envied his *savoir faire.*

Luckily, Dolly was so mild and docile that she was easily satisfied. That afternoon, however, her silence meant she was worried.

"What's wrong?"

"Why did we leave Marcello with that handsome gentleman?"

"That handsome gentleman is a doctor."

"But Marcello isn't sick anymore."

"Yes he is, a little. And the doctor has to see him in order to give him some medicine."

"Oh, then he'll give him back to us."

And with a sweet and tranquil smile she started watching the swans glide on the river.

I couldn't take it anymore. Three hours was too long. It was cold, I had the little girl, and I was in a foreign city. I went back to the office half an hour early.

The nurse or secretary — whatever she was — grumbled that the "session" was not yet over and I had to restrain myself to keep from laughing. To get a grip on myself, I began looking at the books. There were lots of magazines about psychology, hypnosis, and such.

After a while Freud came out of his office with Marcello. He kept a hand on his shoulder, something that annoyed me not a little. The child seemed calm and looked at the doctor with a strange mixture of tranquility and submission. As soon as Dolly saw her brother she ran to whisper something to him, and Marcello replied with a smile. It seemed to me that no one in that room had noticed my presence. Then Freud asked me to follow him to his office.

"What did he tell you?" How many times have I've been asked that question . . . As if it were the key to everything, the magic formula. Nothing so simple! At first he didn't say a blessed thing. He sat down, asked me to do the same, and began reading his notes without a word. I had decided not to make the first move. I was tired of his prima donna attitude, tired of that studied air of mystery. "If he has something to tell me, he will tell me and that's that."

I remember his hands: they were beautiful, long, with tapered fingers — the kind of hands I like, even if a little feminine. Hands of a pianist, my mother would have said. He leafed through a notepad of Oxford paper without looking up. An exasperating rustling. I can't repeat his words exactly; he expressed them in such a contorted, abstract way. In his discourse he referred to Marcello's extreme sensitivity, to his maturity, to the fact that he was unusually intelligent and that this could be a problem. A problem for what? A problem because he had "the intellectual capacity to resist treatment."

"I've never heard of such a thing!"

"Our therapy is not in line with traditional medicine."

Oh, of course. Wasn't that why I had come so far?

From a folder he took out some horrible drawings Marcello had made, the usual caricatures I knew too well. He spoke to me about some of his dreams, of "associations," always in the monotonous and laconic tone of a conductor announcing the next station. Finally, perhaps sensing my growing frustration, he decided to give me his diagnosis. He spoke of "neuroses," of a not better defined "unresolved conflict," but the thing that most seemed to worry him was "Marcello's morbid attachment to his mother" that could lead him to "the destruction of himself" and of the affection of those close to him.

Not a word about the meningitis or headaches. He seemed fascinated by that boy's mind and then he looked at me with almost clinical eyes.

What did attachment to one's mother have to do with destruction? What did I have to do with all this? Well, do you really think I would have gone to all this trouble and made such an absurd trip just to feel attacked like this?

Could he get well? Yes, perhaps, but a lengthy "therapy" would be necessary. It could take months, maybe years. Years? How ridiculous! I heard him, but I didn't listen to him. I didn't care a fig about his "sessions," about his revolutionary methods . . . I understood just one thing: "the destruction of himself and the affection of those close to him." That was all I heard and all I was thinking about. Strangely enough, although I was convinced that the man facing me was little more than a charlatan, I took to heart that phrase, that sort of brutal prophecy. Perhaps that is why I never wanted to talk about it with anyone.

Sandrin certainly didn't embarrass me with questions. I knew I could count on his weakness: he wouldn't ask me anything because he didn't want to know anything. And in fact, from the moment I got off the train he talked of nothing but Titti and the recent follies of Maurras and those other agitators of the Action Française. He was obsessed by it now: he smelled war in the air; he wanted to go "home," he feared "the worst." I played dumb. Much better for him to brood over the fate of the world than my having to give him an accounting of that stupid trip.

In any case, I have to admit that as incapable as Sandrin was of understanding the family's problems, his intuition about politics was almost always confirmed by facts.

His pessimism, however, was so exaggerated that I could never take him seriously. All those stories about the Balkans: Lord help us, they've done nothing but quarrel for centuries!

We returned to Trieste toward the end of 1913, shortly before the war broke out in France. As soon as I arrived in the city I decided

to plan Marcello's bar mitzvah. He was already fourteen years old
and everyone was asking what we were waiting for. To tell the
truth, as long as we were in Paris I had entertained the illusion
that I could get around that obligatory ritual. Religious cere-
monies bored me and I could have happily done without them.
Particularly after that nitwit Marcello declared he was "agnostic"
and said he didn't want anything to do with our ridiculous "folk-
lore." Oh, my, I thought, look what I have to put up with now, and
how can I go on the warpath to get him to do something I care
nothing about? But if I don't make him do it, my sister will never
leave me in peace, not to mention Grandfather Giulio, who the
closer he comes to the end, the more bigoted he gets . . .

> *No importa se gavé sempre magnà taret*
> *No importa se d'ebraico save a pena l'alef*
> *No importa se de Pasqua gave magnà hamez*
> *Idio tuto perdona cò un tempio xe agosess.*

> *No matter if you've always eaten nonkosher*
> *No matter if your Hebrew doesn't go past the first letter*
> *No matter if you eat leavened bread on Pasch*
> *God forgives all when the temple is falling.*

Instead of passages from the Torah, Marcello delighted in
reciting this silly poem his Levi uncle made up partly in Triestine
dialect and partly in Hebrew. He thought it would irritate me, but
instead every time I heard it I laughed right along with him. Basically he was right, but he had to understand that if everyone
expected him to make the bar mitzvah, he had to do it, and that
was all there was to it.

Marcello resumed the Hebrew lessons he had begun in Paris. As
always he was brilliant, but lazy. He liked the language, but he did
nothing but argue about the Talmud. Luckily my rabbi brother-in-
law agreed to help me: we decided to have the ceremony at Venice,
so Marcello could make the bar mitzvah with his uncle who understood him and was inclined to close an eye about the teachings.

My sister, that saint, kept telling me that Marcello was a clever little boy, that he did those weird things just to attract attention, and that Giuseppe had assured her that he really knew the Torah better than he wanted to let on. That might be, I thought, but what difference does it make?

After the ceremony, when I was finally getting ready to enjoy a little peace, Sandrin began saying that we all had to go to Italy before the war broke out there too; that others were already leaving. "Look at the Vogheras, look at the Meiers," and "A good patriot can't stay in the Empire to fight against his own country."

No sooner said than done. Gypsies once again, once again on the road.

Not many wives knew how to adapt like I did; yet they all thought it was normal. No one ever said: "How courageous you are. Always doing everything with a smile, never a complaint, and with that unfortunate son . . ."

We went to Milan first, then to Pegli, then to Genoa. I decided to send Dolly to boarding school in Florence. Otherwise, how would the poor thing ever get an education? Marcello, on the other hand, certainly couldn't leave because of his bad health.

After almost a year of hardship, Sandro finally settled us in the Grand Hotel Méditerranée. I had insisted on going there because so many of my friends were there, and as Sandrin was so often away for work, I didn't want to go on making all those absurd moves alone. Besides that, the children needed a scrap of stability! For Titti I found a new nanny who seemed decent, and Marcello had his usual tutors, who kept getting older, obviously, because the young ones were all on the front.

I was really very happy to be at the Grand Hotel. I had company, and in the evenings there were patriotic meetings and baccarat tables.

People gambled a lot then. Besides, it's normal to look for a little happiness when one is depressed, isn't it? Marcello didn't agree and every time I went to play he lectured me worse than a husband. I had raised a house *donneur de leçons* and the only way to keep from getting angry was to laugh about it.

Toward the end of the first year of war, Sandrin began talking about economic problems. Due to the situation, he said. I wasn't very bothered. It seemed normal for there to be some difficulties. Financial markets could hardly be good at a time like that!

Anyway, the situation couldn't have been so awful, as shortly afterward we moved to Villa delle Rose. Dolly wrote occasionally, but not to me, except for practical matters. Her letters were usually addressed to her father or Marcello.

Marcello couldn't bear his sister's absence and kept repeating that we had a house now, Genoa had good schools, and why did I always want to be rid of Dolly, to separate them?

I don't know how he could get such ideas in his head. It seemed that whatever I did, Marcello had to take it as a personal affront, feeling he was central to every decision I made, and always playing the role of the victim.

In the meantime Sandro was coming and going. And also my acquaintances, friends, and relatives . . . a constant to-and-fro that left me with no one I could count on anymore. Organizing dinners or evening musicals had become impossible. The only recreation left was bridge and baccarat, and even they were beginning to bore me, not to mention the fact that Sandrin was getting more nervous all the time about my losses. As a distraction, I began to organize an evening benefit for the soldiers fighting on the front. This had been the idea of a group of my women friends, almost all busy with the Red Cross, who had insisted on my getting involved. To hear them tell it, I was the ideal person for the money drive with all my connections.

If I was the ideal person, I don't know. What is certain is that I knew to perfection the habits and aspirations of the circle in which I moved. I knew how to attract some and exclude others, how to do it in a way that the Red Cross evenings could soon become an indispensable point of reference for those who wanted to be a part of Genovese society. And besides, *c'était pour une bonne cause*; at least no one would find anything to object to in this. Not even Marcello.

Anyway, to be on the safe side, I decided to involve him in the project. In what capacity was not yet clear to me, but I would find a place for him. Besides, Marcello had started wandering around the house with nothing to do. He read a lot, true enough, and had even taken up smoking — which was certainly not a brilliant idea with his respiratory problems. Dolly was away, tutors had become impossible to find, and Titti was too young . . . The point is that Marcello was bored and I knew that with boredom could come dangerous thoughts. And so I began to take him with me. After all, he was almost seventeen years old. Wasn't that the right age to begin going certain places?

He surely wasn't a conversationalist, but anyway everyone knew he was a bit of a curmudgeon. All the same the girls buzzed around him, apparently fascinated by his ways. My women friends also told me in their transplanted Triestine dialect: "Marcello's certainly not handsome, but there is something attractive about him — his bearing, and the way he seems to be thinking deep thoughts . . ."

But I was embarrassed because he gave the impression of always keeping a close watch on everything. If I ever happened speak privately with someone, he would materialize out of nowhere like the bad fairy. And whenever I danced, he would circle the ballroom so as not to lose sight of me for an instant.

The episode with Giorgio Sinigaglia is just one example out of many, but after that happened no one ever again dared say that my concerns about Marcello were the fruit of my imagination.

There were many Triestines at the Red Cross balls who had fled to Italy like us to avoid being forced to fight on the wrong side. Many of them had not really seen the war, but that wasn't their fault. It was the fault of the kingdom of Savoy that didn't know whether to consider us Italians or Austrians . . . In a nutshell, Italy had taken us in but didn't trust us very much. I knew all the refugees from Trieste in Genoa. Why shouldn't I? They were often longtime friends, even relatives. Giorgio Sinigaglia had gone to school with my brother-in-law Riccardo. We had known each other only by sight, but it was a pleasure to meet and talk about old times. We exchanged news and eventually became good friends. Giorgio didn't dance much at the balls: I'm not a good dancer, he said, but I like to watch the others. Often he and Marcello would be shoulder-to-shoulder with the other spectators, and I would join them.

And so one evening I said to Giorgio: "Let's see if the war is good for something. It might let me teach you to dance at least a little." Giorgio burst out laughing and escorted me to the dance floor. He was hopeless. I don't know how many times we danced — many times, for sure — because, as stubborn as I am, I was determined that "even if he has two left feet, everyone will see how well he dances by the end of the evening!" It was a game, in other words, an innocent diversion. At a certain point I was so tired I had to stop to catch my breath. Marcello remained standing where he was and began speaking very loudly to all present, *à la cantonade*, as he did when he was a little nervous or excited. He said terrible things about "draft dodgers," about all the men who lived the "high life" while "our boys" gave their own lives. He declared he was sorry he couldn't go because of his age and citizenship, because if he could he would be off to the trenches at once. And he might do it anyway one of these days, even with false documents. And to conclude his discourse in an even more decisive manner, he ended by saying that it turned his stomach when he thought about the people who took advantage of Italian hospitality in order to avoid their military obligations and to dance with the wives of those who were instead working for the government.

I stood there stunned, my eyes on the dance floor, while Giorgio seemed more embarrassed for me than for himself. I waited in a stupor for a few minutes to avoid the suspicion that my leaving had any connection with what Marcello had said. Then, with the classic excuse of a headache, I left by myself. As far as I was concerned, that evening my son could go to hell.

From that moment on Marcello's headaches took a drastic turn. Nothing like the past, they were now painful enough to provoke involuntary spasms of vomiting. He would suddenly grow pale and double over; and it was obvious he would never be able to leave the house. The doctors all told me the same thing: it was the consequence, alas, of his childhood illness, but also of his excessive tension. The only thing to calm him was an opiate, such as morphine, but we were at war and it wouldn't be easy to find because it was used as an anesthetic.

Sandrin didn't want to hear about it! Besides he wasn't the one who found himself every day in the company of a boy who hit his head against the wall or gasped in pain, making his every breath whistle in his chest.

It was summer and Dolly was home for the holidays, while Sandrin joined us at the Arenzano seaside resort on Sundays. We managed to find some phials of morphine and its effect was nearly miraculous at first. Lord! I don't know how I kept going during that period, especially since in all that *mismas* I was trying to protect Titti, who was too little to witness certain things.

When morphine was in the house everything went fine. Marcello was able to lead a fairly normal life, even if he seemed a bit confused. He had become less arrogant, and this did not displease me. But something disturbed me, something frightened me about his look, something different I couldn't explain — something sadder, but also quieter. He had a more relaxed expression and at the same time it was more tense, like someone who has had too much to drink and does all he can to pretend he is clearheaded. Some days he shut himself up in his room to read and other times he disappeared for hours without a word. I never asked him where he went, but I knew he didn't meet anyone because he went to his special places around the port, to places that reminded him of Trieste, and where a respectable person certainly would not set foot.

Fortunately (because we thought it was fortunate at the time), Dolly found a way to get the morphine thanks to a Red Cross friend and we proceeded like that, tranquil, like poor innocent fools. Anyway, no one said anything to us, not even the doctors who should have at least warned us; but how could they discuss such things with a woman . . .

Eventually, the nurses who came to give him injections had begun saying they couldn't find the phials; they thought someone was stealing them to sell on the black market. I was furious, but I couldn't do anything. I had to wait for Sandrin to come back, because I didn't want to be the one to deal with the servants. Sandrin came, and in less than a day we understood everything.

If I have had one fault, it is that of being a woman in times when "a lady" must be left in the dark about certain things. Could I have imagined them all by myself? Besides, not even Dolly had a clue, but she was so young it didn't occur to anyone to blame her.

They started talking behind my back, and it was quite obvious that many changed the subject when I came around. As much as I tried to appear indifferent, I was now conscious I had no choice: something had to be done to try to save Marcello and to protect our family's reputation.

Sandrin was opposed, but I didn't care because I knew how to get what I wanted. It was Dr. Segre who gave me the name of the sanatorium, the only doctor who had had the courage to speak to me openly. I had already made the reservation, and for the money there was nothing to do but confront Sandrin with the accomplished fact.

Then there was Marcello to persuade.

I knew that would be the hardest part. And Sandrin had not the slightest intention of helping me: how could he convince Marcello to undergo a treatment when he himself wasn't convinced of its usefulness? Like Vienna. Like always.

Contrary to all expectations, Marcello accepted the idea of the trip enthusiastically. For him, to go to a sanatorium in Bologna smack dab in the middle of the war was a thrilling adventure, the more so because we would be alone. He didn't care about his illness, or even the morphine. Only one thing mattered: I would be away from Titti, my life, and my diversions in order to devote myself to his cure. He looked forward to nothing more than that.

Oh, Lord, what an adventure that trip from Genoa to Villa Banunziana! Endless stops and checks, and each time our having to show our documents — Austrian, besides! — and having to explain that Marcello was suffering from a bad lung infection, and that it couldn't wait until the end of the war, because he needed urgent care. Besides, it was enough to look at him. He was thinner than ever, gray, with a bluish pallor, which according to the doctors was due to lack of oxygen. In spite of that he smoked continually; in fact, all he did was puff away just because he knew that when he went into apnea he would get a little morphine. To help us on the trip we took a nurse, Adelina, whom Marcello pretended to court. What an idiot! Perhaps he hoped it would make me nervous to see him making eyes at that young girl; hardly — for once he left me alone . . .

It took at least three train changes and two car rides to reach the sanatorium. The compartments were full of boys returning from the front and I know what Marcello was thinking when he looked at them. Even before the war he had declared to the four winds how much he wanted to fight: all ideas that were put into his head from reading that fanatic Marinetti. I, on the other hand, seeing those trains pass, only thought how fortunate we were not to be involved in that *mismas*. What good does it do to die at twenty for some stupid war? And I thanked heaven that Sandrin had nothing

more than administrative problems to worry about. All I needed
was for him to be sent to the front!

I had never been in a sanatorium before and I imagined it as a kind
of hospital, one of those miserable places that stink of formalde-
hyde, full of little old people and crabby nurses. And instead we
found ourselves in a kind of deluxe grand hotel. The exterior
reminded me of the Hotel des Bains at Venice, with its white neo-
classical facade. Inside it had a surreal elegance, if you thought
about what was going on outside. There were ballrooms, gambling
rooms, an orchestra, tennis courts . . . Is it possible — I was thinking
— that the period of sacrifice I was prepared to face could be transformed into a holiday, the kind we had before the war?
    The patients were not old at all. Many were my age, if not
younger. They didn't even seem ill, and in fact I quickly discovered that many were there to cure the same "disturbance" that
Marcello had. Not all were as acute, but at that time opium was
very fashionable in some quarters, and the sanatorium was the
ideal place to detoxify without causing talk. All the better, I
thought, because the drug is not contagious, but tuberculosis . . .

I had requested two rooms on the same floor, but not next to each
other. I hoped in that way Marcello would leave me a little space,
even though I knew that it took much more than a closed door to
discourage him.
    From the first visit the doctors had me understand that the
three months of treatment envisaged were not enough: "It takes at
least six to eight months here," they said. "And even then we
cannot guarantee the results." Oh, dear, that's dreadful, I thought.
I would have to send Sandrin a cable, persuading him to wire me
more money, and it wouldn't be easy given the circumstances;
but I had to do it for Marcello, whom I had decided not to tell for
fear of his reaction.

Six, eight months in that place! Very nice, no doubt about it, but I
didn't know a soul. Marcello followed me everywhere I went, or

else he would stay by himself to brood over his customary gloomy thoughts. One evening at the baccarat table I was grumbling to myself about what was ahead of me when I suddenly heard a man's voice behind me: "Gemma? Gemma Levi? What a surprise. Perhaps you don't remember me, excuse me: Augusto Castaldi, Giulio Levi's lawyer. We've met on various occasions at your father-in-law's house, but we're talking about at least five years ago, how could you remember . . ."

Looking at him, I asked myself how could I have forgotten a man like that! Destiny sure enough plays tricks . . .

If it hadn't been for him I really don't know what I would have done. After that evening we started talking more and more often, taking walks, and eating at the same table, with Marcello between us, sulking just to spite me. Augusto had a manner that captivated me completely. I don't how to explain it . . . There was a strength, a sureness about him, and he was so attentive. He understood my every mood change, he cheered me up, he kept saying he had never seen such a courageous woman, ready to face such an unpleasant situation without minding what others said. A real mother, he said, who paid more attention to her son's health than to her own reputation. I liked listening to him talk, with that elegant Italian of his. In addition, he said things that flattered me at a time when I greatly needed support, because the more time passed, the more suspicious I got that I was mistaken again in wanting to help a boy who had no intention of getting well. The doctors insisted Marcello's condition was improving, but to me he seemed thinner than ever, more nervous, intolerant of me and rude toward Castaldi, devoured by a torment he no longer even tried to hide. He was taking less morphine; yes, of course, because they rationed it. But he didn't seem to be getting any better. True, they didn't have to keep him tied to his bed anymore, but how he had suffered to reach such a pitiful end result . . .

Dear Castaldi always did all he could to comfort me, but I was fed up with those fruitless efforts, tired of Marcello's scenes. Augusto said it wasn't his fault, and that he suffered so much. But the truth is that Marcello couldn't bear that I had made a friend, found someone to talk to, to play cards or dance with after dinner. If nothing more, he had quit hounding me. He spent all his time in the solarium, silent, wrapped in blankets, without even reading. I know he despised me. Giacomo, the only friend he made, regularly reported the ugly things he was saying about me: he said that I had taken him there just to get away from my husband and be courted by guests of the sanatorium — all draft-dodging opium addicts and profiteers — while he was the only really sick person there.

In the meanwhile Sandrin wrote begging me to hurry up because the war was over and it was necessary to settle things in Trieste and "you'll see how Dolly has changed and how handsome our Titti has become." And Marcello was also urging me. So I said, "Enough's enough, let's go, because we've done all we can do."

Sandrin couldn't get over Marcello's condition after so many months of treatment: "He's worse than ever. What have they done to him? Why didn't you come home right away if they weren't able to help him?"

Enough is enough, I thought. Let him find a solution, for I wanted nothing more to do with it . . .

Trieste was in ferment right after the war, like a Roman rocket. It would have been lovely to take advantage of it if only we hadn't been in that absurd situation — forced to rent, to fight for what was rightfully ours . . .

In my absence, Dolly had become engaged to a Bohemian, the son of a coffee merchant who had made a fortune in Brazil. A boy, to tell the truth, but sweet. He was perfect for her: rich, from a good family, patient enough to tolerate her strangeness.

Because Dolly was not the same: I had left a self-conscious little Red Cross girl and come back to a girl who smoked, wore her hair down, and amused herself by hunting in swamps in pants and a rifle on her shoulder. It was all the fault of Sandro's weak character, because the day had yet to come when he could say no

to anything! I really didn't care — or rather, I was even pleased
that she was a little more self-assured, but I couldn't tolerate her
becoming vulgar. All those cigarettes and mannish ways!

Titti, however, was unchanged. Certainly, he had grown, but
he was still a nice little boy, affectionate and happy as ever.

My sweetheart, my Nacci.

Everything was fine with Titti. He never criticized, never
judged. He admired Dolly, but most of all he was charmed by his
brother.

After we returned to Trieste, Marcello seemed a bit more tranquil. He didn't go out much, but didn't lock himself in his room
anymore. Often he went to Titti's room to be with him for a
while. Exactly what they did I don't know. Perhaps Marcello
helped him with his homework; at times they would read a book
together. Good, I thought, he's found something to do, and I let
him do it. However, he then started going out and taking his
brother. In the beginning they would take a few turns around the
house: only for a little diversion, he said. Then they began to disappear for hours at a time, without notice. I was not at home in
the afternoons, but I gave orders not to let the young master go
out with Titti. Nothing doing. They always found a way. And
seeing that Marcello paid no attention to me, I had some tutors
come after lunch to break that absurd habit for good.

Anyway, we moved back to Genoa again, partly because we
weren't able to get our house back and I didn't want to stay one
more minute in that disagreeable city. I didn't care about Marcello. He had begun hating me from the time we got back from
Bologna: he's the one who started the malicious rumors about
Castaldi. The more gossip he spread, the more I wanted to be
with the lawyer.

By now Marcello had added opium to the morphine. His
room seemed like an opium den and he was more lethargic, more
listless, and dopier than ever. The only thing we could do was to
keep him in the house and let him be seen as little as possible. He
didn't talk to his father anymore, because he felt Sandrin had
"sold" his sister. Dolly had become inscrutable and we didn't

know if she was happy to get married or not. Why wouldn't she be? Such a proper young man and with a fortune like that.

Castaldi was so maladroit that at times he made me laugh. He worried about my good name and said he didn't want to add fuel to the rumors that were already going around about me. He couldn't understand why I didn't give a fig about the gossip. I was used to it and knew how to silence it. And when I told him that even Sandro made nothing of it, and in fact we often laughed about the foolish things people were saying, he didn't believe me.

I quit worrying about Marcello's sarcasm and his crude attempts to get attention. A decision late in coming, unfortunately, because my war with him had sapped all my energy; it had kept me from seeing who had already made a silent resolve.

But how could I have seen him, my Sandrin, so discreet, always behind the smoke screen so deliberately raised by Marcello?

After Sandro's death everything changed. And maybe it was better that way: as if we were all released from a strange spell. Dolly broke her engagement at once and decided to go to work like a poor nobody.

Do whatever you please, I thought, everyone does what he wants: after such a disaster, what can be worse . . .

Marcello was destroyed by it, and that was natural. He finally realized that someone had suffered more than he. Naturally he laid the blame on me, on Castaldi, on gambling, on my wasteful expenses, on my lack of attention. He, of course, with his rancor and his illness, had nothing at all to do with it.

Augusto and I married a year later, in Venice. A cheerless and hurried ceremony. The children were there; Dolly even came from Davos or someplace in the mountains. During the civil ceremony Marcello didn't for a moment stop rocking from one side to the other, ill at ease, with his hands behind his back. He was so wrinkled he already seemed like a little old man, looking thin and lost in his dark suit.

After the wedding we went to live in Pisa, because anyway no one ever came to see us in Genoa anymore. Naturally, with the debts, the scandal, Marcello's illness . . .

Marcello was calm. He had gone from being too full to being too empty, as if he had gradually been liberated from all those things that plagued him, including his bitterness.

He no longer bothered about Augusto, except for some biting words occasionally — the pale leftover of his former resentment. He was indifferent about everything, even Titti. And if by mistake our glances ever met, he wouldn't even lower his eyes anymore: the truth is he didn't see me.

I had this announcement published in the *Gazzetta*, August 25, 1923:

> From my distressing and unrelenting efforts destiny took you forever. Marcello, this Peace, which you sought all your life in vain, is the only pale comfort to my never-ending sorrow.
>
> Your mama

TITTI

*T*HERE'S A WHOLE part of Marcello's life I know nothing about, obviously, being born eleven years after him — but that's not the only reason, to tell the truth.

To protect me from his dramas, my parents hid a lot of things, and only now can I make sense of much of his behavior.

From the day I was born in Paris until almost the end of the war, I can't say I have many memories. I knew, of course, that my brother was ill, as that was impossible not to notice. Just exactly what that illness was I couldn't say. My sister vaguely alluded to the fact that when Marcello was nine years old he had been attacked by a vicious infection, which undoubtedly affected him all his life.

But that is not what I want to recall about Marcello. I want to tell only about the few years I lived by his side, and about what he let me know of his unusual mind.

His love for me was boundless. My whole family's love for me was in some way disproportionate, as if I were the redeeming angel everyone saw as his own salvation, the Lamb of God who takes away the sins of the world. Exactly as if everyone thought he might redeem the tragedy of his own existence through the innocence of that blond and gentle child who arrived unexpectedly like a gift from heaven. Now it's easy to imagine what a burden such expectations can be to a child. All the more so because I was convinced — with infantile ingenuousness — that I was up to the role fate handed me. It's not that I felt important, but my compliant nature allowed me to give others what they expected of me. And therefore I unconsciously assumed the task of bringing a little consolation to that house marked by sorrow.

For Marcello I was proof of the existence of good, and by contrast, he had to be the incarnation of evil. That there might be an element of self-satisfaction in all this seems obvious to me, even though Marcello was really convinced he carried something malignant inside himself that he hadn't the strength to fight. And so, unable to get satisfying results on his own, he decided to concentrate all his goodness on me, in order to preserve my image, my purity, and to save himself through me.

I understand all this only now, after so many years of thinking about what happened, trying to make some sense of his life, refusing the idea of his having to lose it like that, imprisoned by the slow and ineluctable process of self-destruction, without his life having any meaning beyond death . . .

Marcello was much more than a boy ill with meningitis who died because of his morphine addiction, and more than a tormented soul in the grips of a morbid passion for his mother.

He was a superior being.

Superior intellectually. I'm not the only one to say it; the celebrated Viennese doctor also affirmed it. But superior most of all for his gentle soul, and this is perhaps the hardest part to believe, because most people couldn't see beyond the armor of his presumed "eccentricity," as the specialists of euphemism called it.

I remember his face bent over my bed from my earliest years. Not because Mama didn't take care of me — quite the opposite. In the evening everyone came to my room to tell me a story or give me a kiss, and Marcello always wanted to be the last to wish me a good night. Then, whenever I was sick and had to spend whole afternoons in bed, it was Marcello who kept me company; he who secretly did my homework, explaining enthusiastically his worldview; he whom I didn't want to disappoint.

Ordinarily he would appear in the morning, after I had washed and dressed, before the tutor arrived. Marcello would come in, sit on the table with his back to the window, and begin talking. I remember vividly his sickly profile outlined against the bright curtain, the silhouette of a tuft of hair falling on his forehead, the disagreeable smell of his cigarettes and medicines. Marcello would suggest questions for me to ask, subjects to clarify, objections to propose. He never spoke in a pedantic tone and his talk was never specious. He took my education to heart and had little faith in my tutors.

In spite of that, Marcello never tried to exert undue influence over me. Far from it! He did everything he could to make sure I was different from him. He wanted me to love life; he taught me to be happy, enthusiastic, positive, and curious.

In that short time we had at our disposal in the mornings, Marcello and I discussed and exchanged points of view. He would propose a subject and I would comment upon it — in my own way, of course, and with the logic of my age. But not once did I see on his face that condescending smile often seen on adults at certain ingenuous remarks by children. My brother used to introduce into the discourse some pauses meant to impress — a little affectation Marcello resorted to even with others. It was his way of keeping the interlocutor's attention, creating an expectation, leaving him cruelly in suspense, with an almost sadistic joy. Many times when he did that with me, I got impatient and finished his sentences, stopping him in his tracks. It ended by becoming a kind of game in which the winner was the one who managed to make the first lunge, to unsheathe the phrase that allowed him to advance to the conclusion of the argument. We called it the game of "shortcuts," to which we soon added complicated rules that were best expressed if practiced in the presence of outsiders, totally nonplussed by our unusual exchanges. In our magnanimity, we allowed Dolly to participate once in a while, but given her limited ability and lack of patience we soon decided to exclude her completely from that exercise just for initiates.

During our brief stay in Trieste, after the war ended, the lessons finished at one in the afternoon, and after lunch I was usually full of pep and wanted to do something. But Marcello devoted himself with scientific rigor to his afternoon rest, which was not in any way to be disputed. Needless to say almost every day I sought some pretext for dragging him out of bed.

Through the wall that separated our rooms, I would send him the first message in our invented code. His reply never arrived immediately and at the most it was an irritated grumble.

However, for me that was the first step toward victory, which allowed me to go to his room and subject him to questions:

"Where will you take me today?"

"Nowhere, brat. I'm sleeping."

"If you're sleeping how can you talk?"

"I'll count to three. If you aren't out of here I'll start yelling and Cesarina will lock you in your room."

"You'll never do it."

"Just try me."

"I'm telling you you'll never do it. And anyway, if they have to lock someone in, it certainly won't be me."

"Who, then?"

"You know better than I."

"You poisonous little viper . . ."

His dressing ceremony was never-ending. Marcello chose every accessory with a dandy's meticulous care; he looked at himself intently in the mirror; he posed . . . then, fascinated by his reflection, he assumed strange theatrical gestures. It was a delicate moment, because if I didn't find a way to divert him from his passion for theatrics, it would end by his trying to involve me in some new stylish experiment.

When I finally succeeded in convincing him to forget these artistic fancies and reassured him of his elegance, we moved to the most difficult phase: how to escape surveillance. Mama had given the servants precise orders not to allow Marcello to go out under any circumstance, especially with me. The reason for this confinement was never very clear to me, even if they had vaguely explained it had to do with the state of Marcello's health. But that was not really important. The only thing that really mattered was the success of the operation.

In the afternoons Mama almost always went visiting, and it was actually child's play for us to sneak out without being seen.

What did we do? Neither more nor less than what I had done with my father until a few months earlier: we walked. Marcello, however, never had a precise goal. He didn't want to make me visit churches, galleries, or monuments. We just spent a few free hours together, without parents or tutors around, with the inebriating sense of being involved in some great adventure.

One afternoon with the fierce, cold bora blowing, Marcello irrupted into my room like a fury, excited, feverish. Because of the bad weather, I had just immersed myself in reading the *Corriere dei Piccoli*, absolutely determined, for once, not to put my nose outside. Marcello grabbed me by the arm, fetched my scarf and hat, and, mumbling something to the nanny who came screaming after us, pulled me down the stairs.

He had decided that we should go to the port and so we walked in that direction, hanging on to the ropes. Every step was an incredible effort, and I was so small and lightweight that I was literally blown off my feet. Marcello laughed and laughed, with his strong, liberating, marvelous laugh that I still miss today. He laughed without ever letting go of my overcoat, which he grasped tightly for fear that the bora might sweep me away. When we finally reached the port we found ourselves facing the stormy sea. The waves licked the quays, breaking into a million little drops that created a thick iridescent curtain. Marcello anchored himself to a lamppost and held me tightly. And so, clinging to each other, we enjoyed that incredible spectacle, singing at the top of our lungs a song that Cesarina had taught us:

> It blows high
> It blows low
> Hang on and walk
> It ruins everything
> Wife, what a bora
> Wife, what inferno
> May it go to hell
> The bora and winter!

Mama took a dim view of the climate of confidence that had been created between my brother and me. It annoyed her, worried her. For a while she pretended indifference; then she began inventing pretexts to be more present or to keep me away from him. She dragged me more often to her soporific afternoon concerts or she slipped into my room, sat on my bed, and, pulling an amused smirk, threw a pillow at me, ready to begin the umpteenth pillow fight. We would laugh like crazy, with no holds barred, and Mama would beg me from time to time to be careful of her hair "'cause I just got back from Alfonso's and you're messing it up!" We chased each other around the room, and when he heard the commotion, Marcello would often appear in the doorway to watch us with a pinch of envy. Only once do I remember him taking a pillow in an effort to join us: "Forget it," Mama told him. "It'll only make you short of breath!"

Among the walks we most often took, there was one I detested, and every time Marcello tried to take me there I kicked up a fuss.

Naturally he always found a way to talk me into it. I don't know why he was so anxious to walk in that area. Perhaps he knew those neighborhoods because that was where he went to get his morphine, but I'm not at all sure about that. And I don't even think Marcello took me there with some educational aim or other. The life of "others" had never been one of his preoccupations.

In Rena Vecchia, probably the city's poorest neighborhood, a gang of rowdies often roamed around. If I didn't want to go there with Marcello, it was because every time I got the harebrained notion of indulging him, we landed in trouble. At that time, vulgar and violent little songs that had been the rage at the end of the last century during the Dreyfus Affair were again in fashion. Therefore I was not at all surprised while walking one day on one of those streets to hear the sadly famous "Tananai Figadei." The song ended like this:

> Quela facia da giudeo
> quel muso de smerdocheo
> no xé bon de far salai
> ai, ai salalachai . . .

I had heard it many times, and even if I could barely understand it because of the dialect, I knew it was the kind of provocation that Marcello couldn't stand — "That Jewish face, that shitty mug, can't put salt in his food." Usually, when I spied that gang of boys in the distance, I got scared and begged my brother to get out of there. That day, however, I didn't move in time. Marcello hurled himself at a group of a dozen adolescents, all smaller than he, but much stronger. In the blink of an eye he was on the ground, humiliated, covered in dust, with a black eye and blood streaming from his nose. The boys were generous: "This guy's sick. Best leave 'im be . . ." and they went off yelling: "Abraham, Isaac-o, Jacob go-to-hell-o . . ." For a moment I stood stock-still, not sure which impulse to follow: to run after them or to help my brother. But then I heard him gasping for breath and I bent over to help him up. Marcello turned his back and on all fours he hissed angrily: "Go away, leave me alone! Leave me alone, I said. Get out of here!"

I ran off without turning around, terrorized by the idea of having to go through a neighborhood so far from home by myself. I ran away fast, but not before I saw the tears in his eyes.

❖

For me it is as if my brother died there, since nothing was the same after that. Mama added lessons in the afternoon and afterward, in Genoa, I could never lure him away from his siesta. I would knock and he wouldn't answer. I tried to revive our old codes but I couldn't get a rise out of him. Whenever I went in his room, he would be sleeping, turned to the wall; then he began locking his door, and I don't believe I ever went into that room again.

That was the first big betrayal of my life, the first real sorrow. And in my naïveté, I believed it was entirely due to those tears I saw in Rena Vecchia, and I began hating that stupid pride of his. If only I had understood, if only someone had explained how things were, instead of always treating me like someone who had to be sheltered . . . How many times even today a phrase comes to mind that hurt me then and now seems so clear. Those discourses cut off in midsentence, the angry outbursts against himself, the slammed doors, the sudden attacks of sleepiness. And that time, to make me happy, he had tried again to sing along with me, "Wife, what a bora," and had suddenly collapsed, panting, wiping his mouth with the back of his hand.

My father's death was an earthquake that completely destroyed my childhood illusions, forcing me in a split second to reconsider the whole system upon which I had fastened the certainties of my short existence. I was caught off guard, as though knocked off my feet by an unexpected explosion, prematurely obliged to confront the only pure sorrow: that of a loss once and forever.

That death forced each of us to rethink everything. Dolly, the most independent, chose escape. I, the most ingenuous, understood I had no power over the others; that is, I was not the balance, the element of equilibrium that I mistakenly believed myself to be. Marcello was submerged in feelings of guilt. He, the hypersensitive being, he who could never fit into society because so cruelly wounded by life, was really too taken by his own self-

commiseration to notice anyone else's grief . . . At night I heard
him crying in his room, and I knew that his suffering was different
from ours, more excruciating, because he was convinced he was
the cause of everything.

I don't know if all families are the same, I mean normal families,
to be precise . . . But the fact is that in ours everyone locked himself up in his own little world. We seemed incapable of helping
each other or holding each other in our grief, as though our own
survival obliged us to push the others away. I had lost the Marcello of my happy childhood for some time by now, and I didn't
have the strength or the desire to look for him.
    I looked around me and the only person there was Castaldi.

Marcello observed Castaldi with a kind of hopeless resignation, as
though his arrival in our family were an unavoidable catastrophe,
the just and deserved epilogue.
    I would be lying if I said that I was indifferent to the disconso-
late way Marcello looked at me also. The fact remains, however,
that he was no longer the same person . . . and neither was I.

"Shall we make a photo story?"
    "Leave me alone, Titti. It's years since I've taken a picture."
    "But why not? We had a lot of fun . . . Come on!"
    "I told you not to bother me."
    "Are you still mad about that musket?"
    "I don't care a thing about that musket. Augusto can give you
all the presents he wants."
    "Yes, you are, you're mad about that musket!"
    "It's not the gift that made me mad, but your stupid look of sat-
isfaction when you realized what it was!"

We were living in Pisa and Marcello loathed it. He said it was a
city without a soul, false, a den of decadent nobles and wealthy
bourgeois that he wanted nothing to do with. He pretended not to

be interested in politics, but he had a newspaper delivered every morning. I remember one of his comments about the march on Rome: "Look at this. The Castaldis are now in power. Mama has always had good hunches, you can't deny that."

I had learned over time to do without the walks, but I missed his visits a good deal. I missed our jokes, Dolly's offended air when we excluded her from our games, the stimulation of his observations. Without his sarcasm and free spirit the tutors' lessons had become boring and uninspired, an ordeal. And that smoke, that damned smell of smoke that filled the whole house . . .

I missed Marcello, but I didn't do anything to get him back. Just like the rest of us.

Only a few images of my brother exist from that period.
Only a few memories, also.
I can picture him at the seaside, dressed to the nines, watching Dolly dive from the pier. I remember his gesture when lighting a cigarette off the previous one, and my anxiety when we talked politics with Castaldi. My awkward attempts to make him understand that I was grown up and should be taken seriously. The books that I opened ostentatiously in front of him, trying unconsciously to involve him, surprise him, arouse his approval . . .

In the summer of my fourteenth birthday, Dolly joined us in Marina di Pisa as she always had from the time she left home. Up to then, during those few summers spent together, Marcello and Dolly always managed to dredge up a pale form of complicity that was almost exclusively expressed in a common hostility to Mother, but that year even that feeble reminiscence didn't seem enough.

We were all waiting, more or less consciously, for something to happen. Dolly maintained that Mama was waiting for that moment as a kind of liberation. If she was I can't blame her, because I'm convinced that each of us foresaw that event with anguish, but also with anxiety to finally get it over with. After all, it was an announced destiny and perhaps, in a certain sense, already postponed longer than necessary. Maybe Marcello's destiny, the just one, would have been to die first, and no doubt he would have had died happier.

SANDRIN

DOLLY

*T*HE TEDESCHIS AND the Levis were two prominent families of their respective cities. My grandfathers on both sides
had been, according to talk, feared and respected characters in
their own fields as well as important members of the Trieste and
Gorizia communities.

Sandro was the youngest of three sons, a shy boy, perennially
embarrassed, naive at times to the point of irritation, but sensitive,
and — something fundamental to the family — he had a head for
finance. Early on his father had entrusted him with a job in the
bank founded by his own father and Sandro worked with such
diligence that he could already boast of a brilliant career when he
met Mama.

They met in 1895, during a bar mitzvah in Venice. Both families were present, and all those at the ceremony remember that
Sandro was obviously dazzled by the beauty of that very young girl
barely back from a boarding school in Florence.

Gemma had neither the culture nor the fineness of spirit nor, one
might say, the delicacy of soul of the one who would become her
fiancé, but she had something more . . . an incomparable face
illuminated by rebellious warm, dark blond hair that she tried to

imprison in a complicated and smooth chignon. Her bright green eyes scanning the distance were like reflections of the sea, and every movement of her sinuous body emanated energy and strength, a kind of enveloping warmth that captured everyone she met, even fleetingly. Whoever saw Gemma had to love her; that was the way it was and continued to be for a long time.

When they met, Gemma had just turned sixteen and her father, although he looked favorably on the union, imposed a lengthy engagement on Sandro.

I don't know if his decision came from the reasonable demand to give his daughter time to mature or whether it was the classic paternal reluctance to be separated from her. The fact is that Sandro and Gemma had to endure an interminable engagement. Interminable for my father, of course, who nevertheless coolly pretended to accept it.

Here is how he described it himself on a page in Mama's notebook, the one covered with fine red velvet:

> My adored wife,
> Today is the anniversary of our betrothal . . .
>
> Two years ago, at this hour, I opened my heart to you, my love, and you replied to my rambling declaration, caught up by emotion, with: "I swear I love you very much"; words that clearly demonstrate your noble feeling, so free of deception . . .
>
> Two years, my Gemma!! Two years that were for me like a flash of lightning, having you then, and now, thank heaven, often near.
>
> We are still betrothed, and at least a year and a half must pass before I can make you my wife, but already I promise to be a model husband and father, to love you always (how could it be otherwise?), to be your guide and support.
>
> These words of mine are not simply banal phrases written in an album, but are what I feel.

I wish you all good things, my little wife. Love me
always. Yours always,
                          Sandrin
                          Trieste 7/7/97
                          9 P.M.
                          as a token of everlasting love

Contrary to Sandro's dark predictions, he didn't have to wait
another year and a half before the wedding.

At the beginning of 1898, Sandro and Gemma were married in
Trieste, and nine months later Marcello was born.

What it must have meant for Gemma to leave her loved ones to
follow a man she loved "so much," I cannot imagine. Instead I
can imagine the effort that it took her to be accepted by Grandfather Giulio, a man not famous for his friendly warmth. But
Gemma had a talent for adaptation that allowed her to charm
anyone around her easily and, as much as she was always convinced of the contrary, I am certain she quickly conquered the
Levis also, and along with them all of Trieste.

I was born November 13, 1900. The closeness of the two pregnancies weakened Mama so much that she almost totally relinquished her responsibility for our care. And in fact I have no
memory of her before Cairo. The only mental images I have of
the villa at Trieste involve my father. His good-night kiss, his pats
on the cheek, his playing in the garden with us when he ran
around with Marcello on his back. I remember carriages coming
and going, and maids dashing madly about with ribbons and lace.
I remember the clothes, but not the faces, and of Mama not one
expression, gesture, or caress. Marcello's eyes I remember well,
already freighted with melancholy.

At Cairo the so-called freedom so extolled by Mama was nothing
more than negligence, pure and simple. Gemma was bound and
determined to be part of the colonial social scene and she took us

with her only when our presence could help her with her aim.
She wore dresses of clear, light materials and moved with the
same graceful ease in the dusty streets as among silver party trays.
Papa, enthusiastically involved with his work, enterprising, ener-
getic, looked at her enraptured. In his expression one could read
his perpetual amazement at having such a woman at his side.

After returning to Trieste, Gemma became an even more illusory
figure to me: always in motion, always at the door with her
thoughts projected toward what was coming "next." That is probably why I have no clear recollection of my mother during that
time. I have to refer to photographs to be reminded of her face,
because without them I see only the back of a figure turned away
from me.

While Mama disappeared completely from our existence, Papa
decided to follow our education more closely.
   I have the feeling that the nomad life his work condemned us
to made him feel guilty, and so his fear that our learning might
suffer because of it was manifested in his evening visits when he
meticulously checked the progress of our studies. It was impressive how easily Marcello was able to dupe him, brazenly getting
him off the subject and making Papa believe he had spent all
afternoon bent over his books. I admired my brother and felt
stupid and clumsy in comparison. During Papa's quizzing I
would blush and stammer, incapable of reciting the few things I
had learned. But Father never raised his voice. He waited
patiently, observing my confusion in a kindly manner. Then he
would sit down, draw me close to him, and, stroking my head,
would say to me: "Now breathe deeply, close your eyes, and don't
think of anything. And when you feel calm, tell me what you
learned today." I squeezed my eyelids tightly shut and waited,
calmed by the warmth of those hands somewhat yellowed by
tobacco, in the hope that those caresses would never end, and
sometimes I went to sleep, relaxed and happy on my father's
knees, lulled by the sound of his voice.

When Marcello got sick, in Milan, Sandro became ferocious. I had never seen my father react so aggressively to what was happening around him. He acted like a man possessed. He put a cot next to Marcello's bed in order to be close to him. He didn't go to work and spat out orders all day long, angry with the servants for not bringing water, or with the doctors, sometimes even with my mother, who looked at him as though petrified, incapable of reacting, and most of all incapable of watching her son suffer. Mama didn't go into Marcello's room, but always sent Sandro. And it distressed me that everyone accepted her behavior as something normal.

The fever and delirium lasted many days. Sandro rarely left my brother's room, and when he came out he seemed almost in a hypnotic state. He gave orders, distractedly asked my mother and I how we were, and that was that. He even forgot to come and give me a good-night kiss . . .

"There's a little mousey so neat it'll rock you to sleep, there's a little mousey so sweet it'll whisper good night . . ." Father had made up this silly little song just for me and I couldn't go to sleep without hearing it. I remember murmuring it to myself, in tears, while in the next room Father held Marcello's sweaty little hand.

After his fever began to subside, an analysis of his spinal fluid confirmed the diagnosis: a form of meningitis my brother couldn't survive. Therefore, the day when Marcello finally got out of bed was a great surprise to Dr. Manara.

For all of us Marcello's recovery was my father's triumph. Mama had never been so affectionate with him as she was then. She was grateful to him for having understood her, for having been able to accept her weakness, and above all for allowing her to resume her normal life.

I was proud and happy: finally Father could go back to singing me that song, and Marcello could play with me again.

❖

My brother remembered almost nothing of that period of illness — some fragmented images, some indistinct voices. He peppered me with questions, which I certainly answered unsatisfactorily. When he found out about Sandro's tenacity he was surprised, almost shocked, and in equal measure was surprised by the occasional hint about Mama's lack of courage that the nurses let drop in his presence. That was a reality Marcello couldn't bear, and to remove any doubts about Gemma's love for him, he made every effort to justify her behavior. And so, in order to find the strength to forgive the unforgivable, Marcello felt almost compelled to reject the bond he should have created with Sandro. As if forgiveness for his mother had to go through the condemnation or at least the repression of what his father had done. A distorted reasoning demanded that he refuse the one in order to accept the other, with no compromise possible. And the choice was soon made.

Therefore Marcello decided to attribute to Father the blame he didn't know how to ascribe to Mama, and I am sure that in his heart he preferred to think that Sandro's behavior during his illness was not dictated so much by love for him as it was by his obsessive determination to protect his adored wife. However, I knew it was not that way, and I looked at my brother with a mixture of envy and admiration, wondering how Father would have reacted if I had been the sick one. Would he have come to sleep in my room, or would he have sent the nurses?

When Sandro came that day into the small study where Marcello and I usually did our homework, I knew at once by his uncomfortable and impatient manner that he was about to make an important announcement.

I immediately looked at Marcello, who made a sudden gesture of irritation, ready to greet any news whatever with annoyance. For some time Marcello had frightened me. I was terrorized by the idea that his aggressiveness toward Father would make me have to choose between them one day.

On the other hand, Sandro hadn't noticed anything, or perhaps he was only pretending, who knows. He had remained caring and generous as always, perhaps slightly more anxious, certainly unprepared for such attacks.

He sat down between us, his arms around our shoulders, and began to sing softly, mischievously: *"Paris est une blonde . . ."*

This was his way of announcing our impending move to Paris.

Paris! Father knew how I fanaticized about that city. I had taken to scrutinizing French magazines so eagerly that I was able to describe everything: the *métro*, the *guinguettes* along the river, the steel Eiffel Tower, and then Quasimodo, Jean Valjean, Rouletabille . . . But Sandro didn't immediately notice Marcello's obvious stiffness or the sudden tension that paralyzed me at the precise moment when I was about to give way to my enthusiasm. It took a few seconds, and then in Papa's expression I read his disappointment over our — of my — passivity. And the more I felt his disappointment, the more I hated my inability to liberate myself from Marcello's influence by openly showing the joy my father expected from me.

I don't know how long that painful stalemate would have lasted if Mama had not suddenly entered the study with a radiant expression that Marcello took in at once. One thing I am sure of, however, is that my brother had just invented one of his cruelest tactics: the systematic sabotage of our rare moments of happiness.

His ever more frequent "crises" were also part of the same strategy; in fact, they constituted his sharpest weapon, and Sandro was helpless in the face of his son's wrath, incapable of understanding the reasons for such passion. Every time Marcello started yelling and kicking Papa would look astonished and prudently and silently leave the room.

Alice's Adventures in Wonderland was my favorite book. Both Sandro and I knew it practically by heart. We read a chapter every evening, and Papa loved to enact the Mad Hatter's scene with me. That day, however, I noticed that he wasn't paying attention to what he read. He was concentrating on the illustrations in front of him, as though lost in thought. His distraction began to irritate me, and, sensing my growing impatience, Papa finally asked me casually if I happened to know the reason for Marcello's resentment toward him. That question didn't surprise me very much, but I was annoyed by the idea that my father could be so distracted at the crucial moment of the Non-Birthday, and so I replied, turning the page of the book and without reflecting on the meaning of my words: "Maybe he thinks you love him only because he is ill." That was mean of me. I said it because I hoped it was really true. But when I saw Father's troubled expression, I blushed for shame.

Our arrival in Paris was so intoxicating that for a short while even Marcello, as fascinated as any child by the novelty, forgot his inner battles. Father was absorbed in his work, and his bad French made him feel uncomfortable, incapable of expressing himself as he would have liked.

Gemma, on the contrary, threw herself energetically into her conquest of the City of Light, confident she could use the same ploys that had made her prominent in the little provincial world she came from. And though she could not have been unaware of the veiled haughtiness exhibited by the Parisian *beau monde*, she found a way to convince herself that her social life was a total success.

To make her happy, my father agreed to her Wednesday afternoon receptions at home. Gemma then created around her a little court of expatriate Italians and Austrians, a few members of the French community, the military, and pseudo-artists in search of something out of the ordinary.

And thus, while Mama began to flit again from one drawing room to another, my father devoted himself to me as never before. To indulge my childish infatuation with Paris, every Sunday morning he would take me to visit the places I cherished so. The panoramic wheel, the Argenteuil bridge, the Gare Saint-Lazare, the large department stores: the destinations were all conditioned by my passion for impressionism and the naturalistic novels read with Father. Sandro satisfied my every whim with an amused air, ignoring the sarcastic remarks of Gemma, who lamented the "bad influence on the child" of the many books Father continued to bring me from the library.

In our curiosity to know we avidly read the daily papers. We went to the Champs-Elysées to see the newly arrived Fords from America going down the boulevards as in a gigantic open-air fashion show. Together we discovered a new world that in a few short years had been revolutionized by electricity, automobiles, and movies. Marcello never went with us, and if in the beginning I felt offended by his capricious refusal to share my enthusiasms, I soon understood that his stubbornness would at last allow me to have my father all to myself.

The first time I saw them we happened to be in front of the National Assembly. There were around fifty of them. They waved manikins hanging from macabre gallows over which were inscriptions incomprehensible to me. As soon as Father understood what it was all about, he anxiously took me by the arm: "Walk ahead slowly and don't look up for any reason." I was too frightened by those big loud men not to obey, even though my curiosity to know who they were almost got the best of me. To my questions Sandro replied, "Pay no attention. They won't be here tomorrow. " Only much later did I learn that they were Action Française extremists, involved in the shameful campaign of opposing the transference of Emile Zola's ashes to the Panthéon.

Tension was high in our house during that time. Father was always scowling, irritated with Mama, who didn't seem to take his worries seriously. I wanted to understand what was behind all this and asked Marcello, but his vague answers were not at all informative.
"The press has a campaign against us."
"Us who?"
"The Jews in general."
"Why? What have we done?"

"Nothing. That's just the point."

It was obvious my brother was pulling my leg.

Ordinarily I never got up during the night. But after Mama forbade me to read in the evening I started stealing candles from the kitchen to satisfy my passion without the fear of being caught. It wasn't easy because I had to cross the house immersed in darkness, but that didn't frighten me and no one was ever the wiser. One evening while sneaking out of my bedroom, I saw a light under Marcello's door. That seemed odd because my brother usually turned his light out very early. I slowly opened the door: his bed was empty. I heard strange noises coming from Mama's room. The hallway was dark. I went down it for a way and suddenly grew afraid. I wanted to retrace my steps, but I was turned around, and in my confusion I bumped into something. It was Marcello, curled up in front of Father's slightly ajar door. He was sobbing quietly, crumpled over like a little bird fallen from its nest.

"You will have a little brother or sister soon." In communicating this news to us, Gemma's face didn't reflect the same fierce pride as when she announced our departure for Paris. Of course: two children were undoubtedly more than sufficient for her, and this pregnancy would interfere with her social life.

Mama's lack of enthusiasm allowed Marcello to greet her news with relative detachment, as if it had nothing to do with him. Sandro, on the other hand, couldn't hide his excitement at the idea of having a "Parisian baby," and besides, Mama's pregnancies were wonderful times for him, perhaps the only time when he felt like the legitimate husband of a woman who seemed to be always getting away from him.

That summer we went to Menton.

When we got on the train I remember that Marcello took advantage of the puffing locomotive to slyly imitate Father's desperate attempt to organize the baggage. Marcello had an uncanny knack of imitating the gestures, voice inflections, mannerisms of anyone around him. Caricature was his forte, whether drawn or mimicked, and he knew how to bring out every defect and weakness with cruel precision.

Mama had to give up swimming at Menton, and so Marcello and I found ourselves always alone with the nanny and the Prister children, who had come from Venice to spend the holiday with us.

My father didn't have much use for Dora and Attilio Prister. His intolerance didn't come from personal dislike, but from the fact that he felt uncomfortable with everyone who reminded him of Mama's past life, almost as if he wanted to believe that Gemma's existence began the exact instant they met. However, Mama wasn't bothered by his jealousy and she delighted in telling us stories about when she was a little girl. Then, when Father was within earshot, Gemma relished going into details to provoke him, or perhaps simply to assert her independence. I remember my father's pained look upon hearing her tell me for the thousandth time about when she and Dora sneaked into the men's section in the temple.

Father would listen, red in the face, visibly angry: "I would thank you to stop telling our daughter this stupid story."

Mother would smile, trying to show her scorn, but actually her hand would tremble slightly.

Marcello's worsening behavior didn't allow Father to enjoy Titti's arrival as much as he would have liked. Nevertheless, Sandro insisted on viewing my brother's conduct as a consequence of his illness, to which he could only resign himself. Relations between him and Mama, which were aggravated by his inertia, grew worse. And as much as Father tried in every way to understand Marcello, an unbridgeable gulf had grown between them. Exhausted by Gemma's pressures, anxious to find again that familial peace on which he based his life, Sandro finally agreed to let Marcello see Dr. Freud, confident that after this last of many whims was satisfied, Mama would quit tormenting him.

❖

I am convinced that his initial reticence was due not so much to legitimate skepticism of that new and incomprehensible science as it was to the fact that Gemma would have to go to Vienna alone. From the day they were married Sandro had lived apart from his wife only once, when he had to go to Egypt a few months ahead of us. And he must have felt hurt by the feverish excitement that accompanied her endless preparation for the journey.

After they got back from Vienna the situation took a sudden turn for the worse. Gemma, piqued by her encounter with Freud, now blamed my father for not trying to dissuade her from going. As for Sandro, he seemed preoccupied by some legal problems at work and by the gravity of the international situation. He was distracted, mentally absent, little concerned about what went on at home. Gemma took advantage of it to impose a continual change of servants and tutors she considered too indulgent toward us. It is true that during this period, due to lack of time or will, Father had stopped visiting us in the evening to check on our progress, and both Marcello and I took advantage of it to study very little. As for Mother, after devoting herself — as she said — body and soul to her children, she decided to return to her social life, the only life that allowed her to express the formidable energy of a still-beautiful woman.

And so she took up frequenting theaters and drawing rooms again. She did this without Sandro, who often came home tired and worried after she had already gone out. Something was changing, and Father felt it, because the only thing that had really united them up to then was their obvious pride in being together. Without that grace, that self-assurance as they moved about in society, the "perfect couple" had finally revealed all its flaws.

To escape from his solitude, Father began retreating into Titti's room. That beautiful and serene child brought him great peace, and he stayed there for hours looking at him, caressing his curls, whispering a lullaby. I joined them every time I could and felt an immense joy in exchanging comments with Father about the progress of my delightful little brother. Considering me too clumsy, Mama had categorically forbidden me to hold Titti, and I had to force myself not to pick him up. One day, reading the frustration in my eyes, Father whispered softly: "You can hold him if you like. I won't tell anyone."

At the end of 1913 we returned to Trieste for a short time. Gemma made a real and proper tragedy of it, but actually she must have been happy to be back in the city that had sanctioned her success. She dedicated herself to reestablishing friendships and to taking up her innumerable "cultural" and "charitable" activities.

But the approaching war once again thwarted Mama's plans of conquest, and from her frustration it would almost seem that Europe was breaking in two just to annoy her. Sandro, who refused to fight Italy, wanted to leave Trieste at all costs before the situation got any worse, and he and Gemma had some very heated discussions. The problem for her was deciding which Italian city would allow her to continue her way of life without interruption, and as hard as my father tried to make her understand the seriousness of the situation, as well as the need to go where he could continue to work, almost every evening Marcello and I heard Gemma's desperate sobs, accusing Sandro of "destroying her nerves with his stupid patriotic egotism."

Thus began our pilgrimage of Italian cities: Milan, Florence, Pisa, Livorno. I may have forgotten some. After a little more than a year, Father kept the promise he made Gemma before leaving Trieste, and we settled in a grand hotel in Genoa. God only knows what it cost him to guarantee us a normal existence at a time like that — a life sheltered from the war madness, like an endless vacation . . .

Mama was happy, excited by the inevitable encounters her new life would bring. She had her hair cut modishly, and the curls that now framed her face gave her a younger, bolder look. I don't believe she ever asked how the devil my father, now not working, was able to pay the bills. Nor do I think she ever worried about the emotional state of that almost forty-year-old man, exiled from his city and condemned to idleness while hell broke out all around.

I was now adolescent, and after my parents sent me to boarding school I rarely saw my family. It was during the summer holidays at Arenzano that I began to realize Marcello's desperate situation, and I understood my father couldn't take it anymore.

Every time I think back on that period, at what has been said, at the interpretations that have been given, I feel a great anger growing in me — anger at the three of us who didn't want to see, but also at the others, those around us, relatives, and people more detached who would have been able to do something to stop that madness. But nothing of the kind happened, and Father, tormented by feelings of guilt, by jealousy, by his son's illness, also had to deal with our financial difficulties. That it was his fault, no one doubted: the fault of his weakness, his bad investments, his inability to curb his wife's appetites, his fear of having to make her understand that times had changed and with them they had to change their habits. One time I remember hearing him timidly trying to open a serious discussion about Gemma's relationship with money, and I'll never forget the amused casualness with which Mama managed to switch the conversation to some "delightful" thing Titti had said that morning.

I was the only one, I believe, to be profoundly concerned. By now Marcello was too bent on his own destruction to be interested in that of his family: "*Après moi le deluge*," he was fond of saying when I tried to get him involved, and I think I almost hated him during those months.

I came back to live with the family in 1917, after the move to Villa delle Rose. Then came the morphine, the desperate searches in military hospitals, the money stolen from Father's billfold, Marcello's humiliating quips at the expense of that "draft-dodger" father. And then came the sanatorium also.

When Gemma got an idea firmly fixed in her mind, she knew how to be astonishingly deceitful, and her plan was very simple: to play on Father's feelings of guilt and get his permission to go to a clinic in Bologna. Sandro, who by now understood the inevitability of Marcello's psychophysical deterioration, opposed with all his might yet another useless plan, which anyway came at such an inopportune moment. But Gemma, of course, was always sure she was right and nothing, much less arguments of an economic nature, could make her change her mind.

How many times did I hear Mama declare nonchalantly to some friend, and always loud enough for Sandro to hear: "What do you bet that with his stinginess he'll make us lose him for sure?"

The day Mama left on the train with Marcello, Papa and I couldn't help but admire her. She seemed so proud of her sacrifice, perhaps even a little uneasy, but all in all happy to have found an excuse for ending the war in a flourish.

As he watched the train moving away, Sandro dabbed his eyes with a white handkerchief "because of the smoke," he said, and I pretended to believe him, looking around with a detached air.

The months following Mama's departure were memorable. As a way to economize, I was able to persuade Sandro to let quite a few of the servants go and to temporarily rent out the ground floor of that huge villa. I took care of everything, proud of Father's compliments. His face was lit with an expression I hadn't seen since our walks in Paris. I was grown up, and he realized it.

I read on his face the emotion and also the amazement at the thought of being the father of a young woman so determined and sure of herself . . . I had grown up in a hurry and the difficulties (but also perhaps the desire not to resemble my mother in any way) had made me act a little bit masculine, willful, which my father pretended to find objectionable, even though he was secretly proud. Cigarettes had been the outer sign of my transformation. I began to smoke as soon as Mama left for Bologna. I was little more than sixteen and I went around the house with one of those very long ivory cigarette holders popular then, inhaling the smoke deeply and exhaling it in one breath. At first Papa was opposed to it and we had some lively arguments on the subject. But the more time passed, the less adamant he seemed; in fact, he almost appeared to feel a certain pride in my open indifference to what others thought.

In the evening before supper the three of us would gather around the fireplace. He with his pipe; I with my ever-present cigarette holder. Titti would look at us a little astonished, understandably alarmed by the strangeness of this new situation. By now we had assumed responsibility for his education and we liked to go over his lessons like that, by the fire, jumping unsystematically from one subject to another. We went over his homework and made up some exercises; often Papa would tell one or two little Triestine stories. Then Titti would go have supper with his nanny and Sandro and I would remain alone to comment on the news from the front: the war was about to end and a kind of contagious excitement was in the air.

We exchanged opinions about the last battle, the October Revolution, the Balfour declaration. Palestine was one of the few subjects we disagreed about. "You are Triestine through and through," I told him jokingly in my worst dialect. "You don't trust Theodore Herzl jus' 'cause he's a German Jew."

But even when we were not in agreement, he never treated me with condescension. I don't remember any ironic looks or cutting remarks . . . I stimulated him, or perhaps surprised him. The fact remains that the intellectual complicity that was born between us was a marvelous surprise — but it would be more correct to say a confirmation — for both of us.

In normal families life's milestones are marked by the tragedies, the great and small dramas that sooner or later touch everyone. That was not the way with us. With us, the moments of calm and serenity were the exception. And our peaceful period was drawing to a close. The signs were at first imperceptible, then ever more evident.

I noticed small changes in my father's behavior, but decided not to worry about it. I was too inebriated with what was happening around us, by the idea of soon returning to an Italian Trieste . . .

Only afterward did I learn that during that time the first rumors had reached Sandro of the "improper intimacy" being created between Gemma and Castaldi. Rumors that came to him not from Marcello, as Mama wanted me to believe for a time, but from acquaintances who felt duty-bound to inform my father. Some weeks went by during which Father stopped sitting with me by the fireplace, and his evasive look seemed to announce in advance the last fatal disappointment that he wouldn't be able to spare me.

We returned to Trieste on the eve of the "Liberation" and Sandro tried desperately to put the pieces together. Apparently the situation was much worse than he had imagined: Father was in the grip of an anxiety I didn't understand. But what most intrigued me, I must say, was the fact that he began to ask me to go out with him socially, visibly impatient to introduce me into the Triestine establishment.

We went out especially on Thursday and Friday evenings to visit the elegant drawing rooms of acquaintances and family. I really loved those moments when we were alone on the city streets. To reach the homes of our hosts, we went by carriage or on foot (Sandro loathed the "otòmobil," as he called it, after someone had convinced him that, as it was a French word, it should be pronounced that way).

The most tender and melancholy memories I have of Papa come from that time because, even if we didn't say so, we felt a joy pulse through us at being together, which we knew we had to relinquish soon. When we went to visit the grandparents, Sandro enjoyed telling me old stories about the family, about Giulio's legendary wrath, about the time when the Levis were the most sought-after shoemakers in the city. He embellished his little stories with songs and popular sayings in Ladin. We laughed together when he described the quirks of Grandmother Volumnia, the only one in the family who had not accepted the end of the Empire and who continued unperturbed to speak of "our Francis Joseph of Austria."

Once in a while I could overcome Papa's reluctance and convince him to take me with him to the house of deputy D___, where the intellectuals and entrepreneurs among the Triestine nationalists met in secret. The purpose of the meetings was to prepare the city for what would very soon be its new Italian identity. On those occasions, Father would become involved in passionate conversations about the future of the Triestine economy and finance. Often these discourses gave way to endless disquisitions and I would go to a corner to leaf through the publications of the *Lega Nazionale*. But I seldom remained by myself for long, because Ettore would often come sit next to me. Ettore Schmitz was an old family friend with whom Papa had renewed relations. As a boy Ettore had been much loved by my eccentric great-grandfather, the bank founder, who had always encouraged the fanciful literary ambitions of that creative clerk of a rival institution. My great-grandfather had been one of the few who liked *Una vita*, Ettore's first novel, and from then on the family had been among his admirers. Father had shown me many times the publication on the occasion of Great-Grandfather's golden wedding anniversary in which the young Italo Svevo (so he signed it) had written some very nice thoughts in honor of the long-lived couple: "Oh! You certainly don't say that life is all-beautiful, nor do you look at it through rose-colored veils of illusion! Life is long, and more complicated in duo . . ."

I loved that strange and pleasant gentleman's company, and I believe he was not unhappy to talk with me, either. Especially when his friends grew tired of holding forth on the future of Triestine culture and began to take up more concrete topics that, conversely, left the writer totally unmoved. Ettore would usually sidle up casually, glance over the many books in the library, and finally ask politely for permission to sit next to me. The conversations invariably began with an exchange of opinions about the latest books we'd read, the latest reviews by this or that literary critic, and just as invariably would light on the other great passion we shared: cigarettes.

On the way back home Father often chose the road that ran along the sea. We loved to look at the departing ships, the bales of cloth and wooden crates on the wharves, the coming and going of the dockhands. Sandro seemed particularly attracted by the groups of Corfioti and Russian Jews who passed through Trieste while waiting for a visa to Palestine. He observed those men fleeing from pogroms with a mixture of envy and admiration, as if he too would have liked to escape but couldn't find the courage to leave these shores to go to his Promised Land. With his eyes on the horizon, he was looking at the open sea, and his look traveled from one shore to the other. And from one shore to the other he escaped in his mind . . .

That he would never escape was a certainty for both of us. And with this knowledge I waited in terror for the end of the truce, the moment when Sandro would finally let his ferocious obsession destroy him. Soon his interior battle would begin, the vain attempt to resist the folly in which Gemma's everlasting need for precedence would plunge him. Exhausted and overcome by feelings of guilt, it would be a battle that Sandro — like Marcello — would lose.

That day Father was very surprised to find me in the narrow kitchen of the house where we had moved while waiting for the family villa to be relinquished. Culinary art was not exactly my forte; a girl of a good family was not expected to know certain things, and Mama had not judged it worthwhile to waste any of her precious time teaching me traditional dishes. However, with the war, unearthing a good cook was no easy task, and we were often forced to assume some refugee who stayed with us for only a few months.

It was Rosh Hashanah and I felt I should provide Titti a New Year's Day with apples dipped in honey and the traditional pumpkin cake. So I was in the kitchen, my hands covered with sugar and candied fruit, anxiously following one of Grandmother Volumnia's recipes, when Sandro came in and sat down beside me. He had an alarming expression on his face, and one could read all the shame and the tormented determination to carry out an action completely contrary to his principles. At first I couldn't understand what he was trying to tell me. He was confused and his words didn't make sense. I looked at him dumbfounded, embarrassed by my sticky hands, while he spoke incoherently about our difficulties, about the probable failure of his negotiations to get our house back, and of a certain Enrico, a young Bohemian whose father had made a fortune with coffee plantations in Brazil, and whom I had seen maybe three times in my life in the home of one of Father's friends. When his intentions were finally clear, I felt the world collapse around me: my father was bartering me to save the family, but most of all so Gemma could maintain that social position she had always considered an inalienable right. He was playing his last card, that of renunciation — not only of every affection aside from what tied him to his wife, but also of the moral strength that had allowed him, at least in my eyes, to preserve his dignity up to now. The man before me was not only losing his daughter, he was losing himself.

For long moments I continued kneading.

Thoughts crowded my mind, fogging my capacity to react. I didn't even want to cry; I was thinking only about the cake and of digging my fingers into that orange cream. Father took that kind of mental void for lengthy reflection, and made a brusque and uncontrolled gesture with his hand, perhaps to break the silence.

Or perhaps . . .

I looked at that hand and for a second it seemed to come imperceptibly closer to me. I thought I should wait until it finished its brief move before making a decision. My father's hand brushed mine for an instant, then it sank slowly into the batter and from the batter it went to his mouth: "It's good, not too bitter, not too sweet."

❖

I pretended to docilely consent. I wanted to give Father the illusion of being master of my and of his destiny, at least for a while . . . and in the meantime I tried to convince myself that as much as he was determined to deceive himself, he couldn't hide forever the mortification and remorse that would grow in him.

When Mama finally returned to Trieste, Marcello really seemed much worse. The uneasy glance Father shot me as soon as he saw him confirmed my impression. To the same degree that Marcello appeared to be mentally and physically destroyed, Gemma seemed to be flourishing. Her beauty had assumed something provocative, almost outrageous. I couldn't understand what it was, but for Sandro it wasn't necessary to wonder very long: Gemma was in love and she expressed it with her whole body.

My father was one of those men who considered scenes of jealousy unbecoming and vulgar. Not that he trusted his wife blindly — he wasn't that naive — but he never thought her coquetry would go so far. This time, however, he sensed in Castaldi something different from the usual suitors Gemma was fond of surrounding herself with. Something that could be perceived in the shameless and heedless way the two looked at each other in public.

Sandro was sullen, resigned, still incapable of reacting, but there was a strange determination in him, which I think no one but me noticed, even if I was totally incapable of interpreting it then. Gemma addressed him curtly, sarcastically, almost as though wanting to gauge her husband's passivity, as if she felt a secret pleasure in trampling on the little pride he had left.

Incapable of standing up to his wife, Sandro tried to make up for it by exercising his authority over me. I decided to play along for a little while longer, waiting for him to return to reason, but I was determined to rebel if he pushed too far.

Too shrewd not to understand the reason for my hasty engagement to someone I hardly knew, Marcello reacted with his usual, ineffectual, violence.

On the other hand, Gemma was so enthusiastic she even embarrassed my father. Perhaps because he guessed that her joy was tied not only to the addition of an extremely rich man to our family, but also to the certainty that soon her daughter would go live in another part of the world. Ever since she got back, in fact, Mama felt threatened by me. She had left a little shy and awkward girl, and now found herself with a young woman, unexpectedly pretty, cultured, an able conversationalist. A girl who had been able to create her own personality, who loved to go hunting with a rifle on her shoulder and a cigarette in her mouth, who drove a car and got worked up discussing politics. In other words, a woman who could soon put her in the shade.

I often wonder if Papa was really convinced that I had accepted that marriage of convenience to save the family. When our glances met I read the same unexpressed question in his eyes, as if seeking to confirm something that actually frightened him too.

After we returned to Genoa, Gemma and Castaldi — who by chance now worked for a firm at nearby Pegli — became a couple. On the surface it seemed completely natural, the more so since my father hadn't gone out with his wife to concerts or salons for some time. But his closest friends understood that it was something else, and they already spoke of "poor Sandro" in mocking tones usually reserved for *maris trompés*.

After repossessing her Villa delle Rose, Mama got it in her head that a family like ours shouldn't continue going around in a carriage. And so she became the owner of a Daimler, "our Daimler," she always said with pride. The latest whim, the latest senseless folly . . .

Gemma led a frantic life: involved with her receiving day, the *jours* of others, the box at Carlo Felice Opera, the meetings with the literary society, and endless charity work with the Israelite Commission; not a moment left over to take into account what was going on in her own house.

Sandro, meanwhile, could no longer extricate himself from

the net being woven around us. In order to avoid usury he had to ask his uncles for loans. The unsound edifice he had built was collapsing around him: he had lost Marcello's affection and esteem, his wife made fun of him, he had offered his daughter to the highest bidder, and he was no longer in a position to support his family.

He rarely went out; he stayed holed up in the study or library most of the time. What he did closed up there for hours God only knows. The only person he was still happy to see was Titti, probably the only one who didn't make him uncomfortable with inconvenient questions.

As for me, I did nothing to get close to him. I wanted to punish him, make him beg my forgiveness, force him to backtrack. We looked at each other with suspicion and discomfort, each waiting for the other to give in.

True, he could have saved us from that macabre performance, though at times I wonder if that sin of pride might not have been the only sin he never allowed himself . . .

There was a flash of triumph and scorn in Gemma's eyes when Sandro told her in an offhand way that, in addition the usual guests, he would also be happy to invite Castaldi to dinner. To have forced her husband to accept her lover in their home constituted a definite victory. I was despondent. I couldn't figure out if Papa's weakness was really the result of cowardice or, as I had wanted to believe for too long, the result of his goodness of heart.

When we gathered together around the table that awful evening the uneasiness was palpable. Not even cynical Marcello could behave with nonchalance. No one seemed capable of starting a conversation. Gemma herself appeared to be suddenly aware of the impropriety of the situation and tried to repair that terrible error by a show of exaggerated gaiety that made things if possible, worse. Sandro, on the other hand, was extremely calm and reflective. He spoke little, but always politely. I remember that he even made the effort to open a discussion about D'Annunzio's conquest of Fiume, a subject everyone at that time felt he had something intelligent to say.

I didn't say a word and didn't look at anyone. I felt very ashamed to be sitting across from Castaldi, near my father. My poor "fiancé" did everything he could to get me to smile, which only resulted in increasing my irritation, and I would have quickly become completely hateful to him if my father had not suddenly stood up with the pretext of giving the maid an order.

I was the first to jump to my feet, and the first to go in after someone — who knows how — broke down the door that was locked from inside.

The blinding white enamel of the bathtub, the trails of dark red blood that ran straight, slowly, almost parallel.

At first I didn't even see him . . .

Only that white and those red stripes.

Then I noticed his feet quivering, like a fish quivers after the hook is removed. Actually his whole body was trembling. Not a sound, only those violent spasms. I stood watching that unconscious scuffling for some time. And I remember thinking clearly: poor Papa, he couldn't even do this well.

Sandro died after two hours of agony.

He left this note for us:

> I ask Gemma to make a new life.
> I ask Dolly to begin hers: may her marriage be blessed.
> And to all my dear ones, may you find the strength to pardon me.
> *Baruch ha Shem . . .*

Sandrin

GEMMA

*I*T MUST HAVE been around 1895. It was certainly my first
ball, because I was usually taken home right after the bar
mitzvahs. But on that occasion my papa must have thought it was
time to let me make my entrance into "society," after finishing
boarding school. The ritual was in honor of the son of a family
friend, David Luzzato, a little bit stuck up, but my friend Dora
liked him a lot. Luzzato was from Trieste, but for some reason the
ceremony was held in Venice, at the Scola Grande. Dora and I
managed to get a seat on the first row in the women's gallery that
overlooked the men's section. Every time we bent over the railing
to steal a look down, the old women behind us would hit us with
their canes to make us straighten up. Mama smiled but had to
appear indignant to avoid her aunts lashing out at her. Dora and I
counted the minutes separating us from the reception. The temple
was a real bore for us and we always pretended to pray by moving
our lips. I never knew when it was time to quit looking at the Ark
and was in a state of tension watching what others did, ready to imitate them as soon as they moved. I have to admit, though, that the
temple was very beautiful with all that gold and those red drapes,
and I remember thinking that I would like to be married there.

❖

There were many people from the Trieste community at the reception. My parents knew practically everyone, because even though they had only recently left Gorizia, they already had an important position in our new city. Dora and I stayed together talking and laughing like two idiots: in other words, doing what girls do. We were exceptionally pretty, no doubt about that. All the boys wanted to dance with us, especially with me, I must admit, because I was very flirtatious, which was not surprising since the only things I knew about courting I had read in those few frivolous books Mama gave me permission to read. I don't remember Sandro, but Dora and Mama always told me that was where we saw each other for the first time. It could be, but I met so many people that evening!

What I remember is that we met in Trieste that same year — in the Ravennas' home, I believe. By that time I was a little more experienced and paid more attention to my dance partners. Sandrin didn't come forward at once, because I had the first dance with Prister, the one who later married Dora. I was distracted and excited by all the goings-on, and I loved to dance. I was also rather good. Well, I've always been, because when I dance I don't think of anything else, and I'm never inhibited by shyness. Sandro had reserved a tango, the only dance where my talent certainly couldn't shine, because it is so rigid and codified. I just couldn't let my partner take full control, which is fundamental with the tango. Sandrin danced it divinely, with class and elegance! When he held you, you wanted to let him carry you away with him. I was thoroughly impressed. Not so much by him, however, as by the way he danced. In fact, I paid no attention to what he looked like.

In those years we divided our time between Trieste and Venice, where my sister lived. My sister Eugenia was married to Rabbi Giuseppe Bassi, a very dear man, but so poor. Papa had arranged the marriage because he was keen on having a rabbi in the family, and had given his first child in marriage without asking her opinion. Fortunately, my sister was a sensible sort and saw nothing to protest about.

I, on the other hand, was terrified of ending up like her. And I kept telling Mama: "I don't want Papa to make me marry someone I don't like and furthermore who's as poor as Giuseppe. I'll choose my own husband and you'll see that I'll make such a good choice that Papa won't find any reason to object."

To someone like me raised in Gorizia, Trieste was the center of the world: a cultured, elegant, wealthy, and mysterious city. Alessandro Levi came from a well-known family of bankers or moneychangers who had made their fortune with the free port. But as my father was a scientist he didn't much like those "money-grubbing" types, even though he knew very well that such a prejudice would not be sufficient reason for refusing a good match.

Sandrin was such a dear! When he knew I was in Trieste, he would announce his afternoon visits with a calling card. However, I was not often home and he had to resort to a thousand tricks to find out where to track me down. His perseverance was remarkable. And I thought: a good-looking, wealthy, cultured man from a good family. Pay attention, Gemma, things like that don't come along every day! And even Dora said: "As soon as he asks you, you've got to say yes, so your father won't be able to do anything."

The day he proposed we were at a very boring afternoon musical. One of those concerts you don't dare miss because everyone is there. Sandrin went early and was waiting at the door for me to arrive. I met him with a lackadaisical attitude, but I had noticed for some time that things were changing, and that perhaps the moment was drawing near. I was very excited, with my heart pounding with anxiety. I had never been in such a situation and didn't know what to do. I was laughing with a friend when Sandro came up to me, asking, in a low voice, if I would like to see a certain picture in one of the rooms. I followed him and tried to look interested, still in the grip of that stupid giggling fit.

Then he stopped and said:

"How beautiful you are, Signorina Gemma, so unrestrained . . ."
A foolish thing to say, I thought, and felt like laughing again.
"You won't get it into your head to try to tame me?"
"Tame you? Oh, no, quite the opposite. I would like to see you
laugh like that forever."

Suddenly I was afraid. I thought: this must be a proposal and if I
say yes I'll become his wife. And then? I'll have to stay with him
for the rest of my life. The rest of my life. That's hard to imagine
at sixteen . . .
My head was spinning.

I don't remember what happened next, whether I was standing or
sitting down, whether I was embarrassed or nonchalant. I only
know that I said something that seemed like consent; then I
talked to Mama who talked to Papa and that was that.

All told, it wasn't so simple. Because I was little more than a child,
my father and Giulio Levi agreed to impose on Sandrin an
engagement period of at least three years.
The nicest years. As a fiancée I went to all the receptions with
Sandro and a chaperon, proud to appear at events by his side.
Sandro was a very handsome man, but — more than handsome
— he had an imposing bearing that drew attention. Black hair
with a long and slightly curly mustache that he kept smoothing
with an odd gesture of his left hand. He was only three years older
than I, but he already seemed like a man and sometimes his seriousness made me a little uneasy.

Ordinarily he came to visit after five in the afternoon, but one day
he came a couple of hours early for some reason. We lived in an
apartment on the second floor, along the sea, or rather, with the
windows high *over* the sea. Mama had passed on her passion for
water, swimming, diving to me: an unusual activity for those
times, which in our house was always strictly a female specialty.
Mama and I would dive from the living room window directly

into the water. We started doing it from the time we arrived in Trieste and Papa, who understood it would have been useless to argue, restricted himself to going around grumbling that we were two brainless fools and "what had I done to marry an irresponsible woman who drags that poor creature behind her!"

Sandro routinely came in a carriage, but on that nice warm day he decided to take a walk. When he reached the house he heard a splash, and looking in the water, he noticed a little black dot appear in the distance. He was about to remove his jacket and jump in with the intention of "saving that poor wretch," when he heard me laugh, and, looking up, he saw me at the window in my bathing suit, ready to follow Mama. How many times he told that story, and as no one believed him, he would proudly embellish details in order to boast of the singularity of the woman he had chosen to marry.

I was still a girl and unable to take things seriously. The day of shidduchin, my parents gave me a thousand instructions, asphyxiating me with their anxieties and worries. I had asked Mama to let me wear my red dress, but she made me put on my cream-colored one. I asked to change my hairstyle, but every proposal I made was rejected without any possibility of argument.

As soon as I entered the room where the Levi family was waiting, I took my place. I looked around curious and impatient, looking for some gesture that would begin the ceremony. We all seemed a little ridiculous, to tell the truth, and I must admit that, as often happened to me in important moments in my life, my mind would follow thoughts totally unrelated to the situation. At the precise instant when Sandro officially asked me to become his wife, I heard a ship's siren in the distance: "The *Marseille* has set sail!" I shouted, dashing to the window.

Sandro had to simulate a coughing fit to keep from breaking into laughter, and my future in-laws didn't even try to hide their embarrassment.

On the way back home Father flew into a rage. He said I had no respect for anything: "You want to be a lady and you still behave like a little girl. You've given the Levis a very bad impression, and I can just imagine what they think of us now. I shouldn't have listened to your mother . . . I knew you weren't fit to take out in society!"

I loved Papa a great deal, but I wasn't bothered because I knew he would complain and then forget about it. Anyway, there was little to argue about now. I was officially engaged and soon I would be Signora Gemma Levi.

Gemma Levi . . . that has a nice ring to it, I thought.

If it had been up to me, the engagement would have lasted an eternity. I liked feeling myself courted, looked at with envy by my girlfriends, and I liked all the presents Sandrin gave me, and the poetry. At times, true, he was a little asphyxiating because after all we were not yet married. But for him that period was a real hardship. He suffered and I didn't understand why: we saw each other every day, we went to the opera at the Teatro Grande together, we attended the same salons. In a nutshell, I felt like we were already married. And yet this was not enough for Sandrin; he would have liked for me to be by his side every minute.

To my great surprise, it was my father who decided to push the wedding date up. I think he had given in to pressure from Giulio Levi, because they had just made a trip together.

Papa was an esteemed mathematics professor, and the senior rabbi had decided to send him to the Jewish international assembly at Basilea in his capacity as a member of the Gorizia Community Council. Levi was required to attend as one of the three leaders of the Trieste Council. Aside from questions related to Zionism, they obviously had talked about the wedding of their respective children. Papa was not interested in Herzl's plan, and apparently Giulio seemed very skeptical too. I don't know how much this drew them together, but the fact remains that as soon as my father got back from the trip, he told me that after his meeting with the Jewish assembly in Gorizia he would set a definite date for the wedding.

❖

Mama kept saying that this was a very important meeting, because if Papa could persuade the others, his influence with the community in Gorizia, which he had neglected since we came to live in Trieste, would be strengthened. I didn't understand his interest in Gorizia's community, but when Papa got an idea in his head there was little room for argument. I only remember that the day when he went to deliver his speech he was very excited and Mama kept telling him: "Be careful or with your heart it might end badly!" As if to feed her anxiety, Papa replied that if he couldn't make them understand that Zionism was a socialists' thing, it would end badly just the same. He had it in for young people, the Russians and the Greeks. He said that if they hadn't been able to make themselves accepted, there might be a reason for it, and that it would be absurd to make enemies of the Austrians, who for thirty years behaved more than well just to please those people.

In his enthusiasm he didn't notice that the topic was of little interest to us. More than anything else, Mama and I were thinking about the wedding, and we couldn't wait for him to finish this story so we would finally know the date.

The meeting was to take place on a Wednesday afternoon. Papa left assuring us that he would be back "within a few hours," but he didn't get back until nearly nine in the evening. It had all gone well, better than he had expected.

From the meeting it had clearly transpired that other community members were also afraid the Zionist talk could do more harm than good. We had nothing to worry about. From the time of the emancipation no one had bothered us. We weren't in the France of the Dreyfus Affair!

"What is this Palestine?" they said. "It's enough to have to fight for Italy. What's Palestine to us?" An overwhelming majority decided not to finance local Zionist groups, thanks also to Giulio Levi's intervention. "You can't imagine the talk he made. All things I wish I had said, and they just came pouring out of his mouth."

A copy of his talk had been distributed to the audience and

Papa was anxious for us to read it. It was so admirable I saved it. It began like this:

> Herzl is a lay utopian, a socialist idealist, a man who — he admits it himself — doesn't know a single word of Hebrew. He wants to use the community for political ends. But our community in Trieste is already in jeopardy: look at all the mixed marriages, look how many people have left us to embrace the so-called religion of the fatherland, not to mention the *Konfessionlos* who disavow their religion. And yet, all the Jews of the eastern Empire and the Balkans seek refuge in Trieste. Those Corfioti come to us en masse, and why? Because we've managed to get what we wanted. Because we are free: we live, we work, and we practice our faith freely. Do we want to be ingrates? Do we Triestine Jews want to follow a Hungarian atheist who preaches the establishment of a new state whose language will presumably be German? I know that some council members look on Herzl's plan favorably, but I invite them to reflect on the consequences that such a choice would have, not only on the harmonious equilibrium between our community and the society that gathers us to its bosom, but also to the preservation of our traditions, our culture, our faith . . .

On rereading those words, Papa's eyes grew moist. As he folded the handout, he looked up at me and said: "I'm so proud you're becoming part of that family. Of course the German language wouldn't bother me, but everyone knows Levi's on Italy's side. Still, it doesn't matter; I like him just the same."

Two months later, the wedding took place. I would have preferred to be married in Venice, because the temple there is much more beautiful, but Mama decided that it should be Trieste, and she had the last word.

❖

When I arrived at the temple the sky was overcast. The carriage stopped right in front of the steps because Mama was afraid I might get my dress wet.

The Scola Grande was already so full that the idea of being the center of all those people's attention made me more nervous than the ceremony itself.

Stock-still in front of the bimah, Sandro was waiting for me, tapping his foot as though beating the rhythm of a melody only he could hear.

He looked so handsome in his dark suit with his white tallith and gold embroidered kippah. We made a wonderful impression, there's no denying it . . . a perfect couple.

Sandrin was so emotional he couldn't even look at me. Then, at the moment of the kiddush, his hands trembled so badly he nearly dropped the ring: "By this ring you are bound to me according to the Law of Moses and Israel . . ."

I don't remember how that sentence sounded in Hebrew, but when he pronounced it, I automatically extended my hand on hearing an incomprehensible word that the rabbi had indicated as a point of reference, and the wedding band was slipped next to the marvelous opal surrounded by diamonds Mama had just given me. The chuppah dangled above us like a sail and Sandro and I held each other tightly under that symbol of our union.

I don't remember much of what happened afterward. I saw blurred faces smiling around me, the rabbi's bobbing head, the inlaid work of the Aron Hakodesh, the candle wax dripping on the menorah, and then the monotonous voice of the witness reading the marriage contract. A little later, Sandrin squeezed my arm hard because I was totally rapt: it was time to sign.

The contract . . . I had a dizzy spell, but no one noticed, and I never knew if emotion or my tight corset caused it.

After leaving the temple, the guests gathered around us. Sandrin and I were literally propelled to two chairs and raised by that crowd of friends and relatives. We held on to each other's hands.

The chairs were rocked back and forth in rhythm to the music as we were suspended in air. Sandrin was terrorized by the thought of falling and kept yelling: "Careful, be careful!" But I wasn't worried. My elation finally infected Sandrin. I know because when I started singing with the others I turned to him for a moment and got a fleeting image of my husband smiling happily.

All Trieste was at the reception, and the carriage traffic in front of the Levis' house was endless. Sandrin and I weren't able to say a word to each other because there was always someone wanting to congratulate us. Mama stood beside me and softly whispered the names of those I didn't know, whom by then I was greeting like a robot. Occasionally Sandrin would cast a desperate glance at me, and I made a resigned face.

Then came the dinner and dance. Milly sang something with Maestro Banfi, while people continued to come and go as though taking turns, and the house was never empty.

Calm at last. We were exhausted. Everything had gone perfectly and we knew our wedding would be the talk of the town for a long time.

Sandrin was so sweet. More nervous than I, certainly. He didn't know where to begin. When we were alone in our new house, I suddenly felt very sad. I missed Papa and Mama. It was as though only then did I understand that a phase of my life had ended, that I would never again see them as before. I cried and Sandrin looked me sympathetically, whispering words of comfort, while he held me tightly and caressed me. Then, gently, he led me to the bedroom:

"I can sleep in the other room, if you like."

I took his hand and bathed it with my tears. Then I kissed it and quietly asked him to stay with me.

We came back from our honeymoon after barely two weeks, the amount of time old Levi allowed Sandrin. "Money doesn't grow on trees," he said. How I hated them, all those maxims.

Sandro worked long hours, and I became a little bored all alone in that big house. It was beautiful, for goodness' sake, but decorated entirely with the Levis' taste, full of English furniture and dark drapes. Oppressive.

"Do you like this room, Sandrin?" I would ask him occasionally, and he would look at me surprised: if there was one thing that meant absolutely nothing to him, it was room decor. He would respond with a tender smile, and unfailingly encourage me to do whatever I liked.

I had a little Venetian sitting room made and furnished the *salon de compagnie* with some beautiful black boulle with gold fringe. For the dining room I chose a Biedermeier buffet and I would have liked to have a rococo *salon de famille*. As for the rest — the servants, running the house — these were things I'd rather not do. That was no fun. Grandmother Volumnia didn't understand this, and neither did Mama, but luckily I didn't have to listen to her at least. Volumnia, on the other hand, complained — not so much to me, because she understood it wouldn't be worth the trouble — but to her son. And Sandro relayed those things to me with embarrassment, apologizing almost as though he were to blame. I would reply, ironically: "Just a minute now, are you sorry I can't pick a gardener?" and he would hedge, saying he hoped I would never turn into one of those women who spend their afternoons making lace and talking about cooks and coachmen.

I wasn't feeling very well, and after a few days I decided to go to the doctor with Dora. The verdict was what I had been afraid of: I was pregnant.

I didn't tell Sandrin right away, as if not talking about it might postpone the reality for a while. On Tuesday, after the usual visit with the Venezianis, Sandro decided to stop the carriage for a walk along the sea. It was there I told him, on the Rive, in the dark, so he wouldn't see my face and realize my consternation. Sandro held me tightly and swung me in the air. And while he continued to shout his happiness to the world, I was thinking about everything I would have to give up.

During those weeks there was much agitation in Trieste brought
on by the articles in the *Piccolo* about the Dreyfus Affair, and
Sandro, who was a good friend of Teodoro Mayer, could talk of
nothing else. I didn't care a fig about Dreyfus. In fact, just the idea
of that unpleasant French officer was irritating. But I was surprised that even old Levi, in spite of his dislike for the Empire,
had taken to criticizing the Irredentist journalist: "A fine thing,
your Teodoro, who converted so he wouldn't have to pay dues to
the community. Congratulations."

The *Piccolo* had even organized a student demonstration, and
I remember that Sandrin would have been a willing participant if
Giulio hadn't forbidden him to leave the office.

Mayer often came to our house to talk with Sandrin, and
whenever I felt bored and stood up to leave, Sandrin would try to
get me involved: "Is this really so uninteresting to you? It's a
matter of our future and the future of our children . . ."

"Come now," I would say, "even Papa says it's all an exaggera-
tion of that crackpot Herzl . . ."

We had discussions, and I must admit that I was flattered to see
how much Sandro cared about my opinions about topics that
were usually not discussed with a woman.

I was pregnant, but I felt well. As there was no reason to change
my habits, I continued going to salons or to our box at the Teatro
Grande, or Milly's evening musicals. Sandrin always went with
me, and even when he had to work late, he managed to meet me
so we could go home in the carriage together. We often went
along the sea, even if it was a longer way, but we liked to walk
along the Rive at night, with the carriage following behind. I
remember those nocturnal walks well. I remember holding on to
Sandrin's arm while he asked about my day; I remember the
pleasure it gave him to listen to my stories.

As a young wife I often went to visit him at his office in the bank
close to the stores where I usually went shopping downtown. I
liked watching him work while he dictated letters with his pipe

in hand, or while he took notes at the telephone, raising one eyebrow as he always did when concentrating. As soon as he saw me he left everything where it was. I sat on the edge of his desk and jokingly told him about Dora's latest gaffe, or I showed him a sample and together we would choose a pair of gloves. But very soon I had to give up those visits, because old Giulio, unable to restrain his disapproval, would go down the hall grumbling: "A woman in the office . . . It has never been seen! And pregnant besides! Fine that we're all modern now, but the fact remains . . ."

On Thursdays, Sandrin always arranged to get away in time. And I was very keen on having him beside me when receiving the guests. We would go downstairs before five o'clock, when the first guests began to arrive.

I usually stood near the fireplace, since the music annoyed me, but I enjoyed chatting with everyone a lot. On the other hand, Sandrin was perfect; he would go from room to room, careful not to neglect anyone. Every once in a while he would reappear, and passing by me would brush my shoulder or cheek with his fingertips; or he would lean against the doorway and look at me with his pipe in hand, the smoke partially covering his face. Dora, who always had sharp powers of observation, went into ecstasies: "It's quite impressive, Gemma. I've never seen a husband so in love. You are certainly a most fortunate woman."

With advancing pregnancy, my big belly naturally began to be an inconvenience. I pulled in my corset, I bought new dresses, but nothing fit anymore. Sandro teased me by saying if I kept on tightening my corset like that, the poor child would be born an idiot. I had to give up, and so the last two months I didn't go out at all.

To help me combat boredom, Sandro came home as soon as he could. He would sit on the bed in his overcoat, bringing in an irritating odor of cold, and ask me a thousand questions. His concern made me nervous. I felt alone, confined, unable to move about freely. I looked at my body and didn't even recognize it. Sandro tried to reassure me: I was still the most beautiful woman in the world. Wherever he went, he heard people speak admiringly of me, and our friends were all very anxious for the baby to be born . . . Lucky them, I thought, I'm certainly not in such a hurry!

The midwife found it amusing to tell me over and over how Sandrin had stayed outside the door the whole time, frozen stiff. I don't remember a thing . . . I can still see Sandro afterward with the baby in his arms, trying to give him to me, but I refused to hold him. "Don't be afraid, a mama can't hurt her baby." But I was sure I would drop him on the floor, he was so tiny.

    Sandro seemed beside himself with joy when he held Marcello. He sang him songs, talked to him. This was his son, the male child, and I knew it was important, and I thought with relief: fine, even if we have only this one child, I've done my duty.

The Brith Milah should take place eight days after the birth of a male child, but Marcello was still so small it seemed completely unwise to me. I was not the most knowledgeable person about rituals, and besides we were all girls in my family and for that reason I knew little or nothing about circumcisions. Anyway, Sandro wasn't religious either, and so I didn't understand why it was important to give in to that barbarous custom. "If he's not circumcised he's not Jewish," Sandro said, which made no sense to me. He is Jewish because he's the son of Jewish parents. That's all that matters.

I gave up in the end. I was too tired to argue, and Sandrin organized it all by himself. The sandak would be his brother Riccardo, and that was fine with me, as if I cared! The mohel of the Grand Temple had insisted on shaking my hand before the ceremony. He was a nice-looking old man with gentle ways. However, I refused to take part in the ritual. And I didn't want to see Marcello before or after it. I wanted it to be clear to him also that I had nothing to do with that torture.

❖

From the time Marcello was born I cried constantly for no reason. I still felt weak, tired, and terribly sad. When they brought the child to me I looked at him with amazement, curiosity, and, most of all, absolute detachment. Sandrin tried to calm me: "Look, it's normal. It's painful to have a baby. You'll love him when you feel better, you'll see."

That could be, but in the meantime I felt like a monster.

I even felt a little envious of Sandro; it seemed so easy for him. To take the baby in his arms, to cuddle him, to smother him with kisses: all things completely unnatural for me.

A little later we took a trip on the Carso, near Monte Maggiore where the Vogheras had a beautiful chalet. Sandrin got it into his head that the fresh air and brief separation from the baby would do me some good. This way I would miss him, he said, and when I got back I'd no longer be afraid of holding him. I was a good walker, while Sandro, even though slender, certainly did not have an athletic build. He plodded along and soon got tired. Often I would surprise him sitting on a tree trunk to catch his breath: "You're really a big lazybones, my poor Sandrin." He would shrug, embarrassed like a child caught in the act of some mischief. Evenings I played baccarat with our friends while he read beside the fire. He didn't like to gamble, but in those days he still enjoyed watching me, because I lost patience when I didn't get good cards, and I hated to lose.

When we returned from the mountains I felt much better. Marcello had grown and that made me less afraid. Also I had recovered my energy and seemed almost back to what I was before. I was so happy to be able to wear my new clothes, to go around town without feeling so awkward . . . But it was a short-lived joy, because exactly nine months after Marcello was born I got pregnant with Dolly. And it started all over again.

I nearly went crazy. At the doctor's office I had a real hysterical fit.

It was exhaustion, everyone said: "It'll pass. Well, yes, of course it's difficult. They are a little too close . . ."

Sandro understood that the two pregnancies coming one after the other could be the end of me. So in the sixth month he got the idea of sending me to Venice, to my mama and Eugenia. At first I didn't want to go, because my sister was so irritating, always praying and not eating this or that. But in the end I decided that maybe a change of air would do me good, and Mama knew how to lift my spirits. "Me, too, when you were born I was so tired I didn't even want to hear about it. But you'll see it passes, you'll forget about the pain; and anyway the second one is easier. You'll see."

She was right. Dolly's birth didn't sap my strength, and I was happy to have a girl. It tickled me to think about little dresses and hairdos for her. She seemed like a doll. Plump, with those little curls and that little pouting face. Sandrin definitely lost his head. As soon as he came home he would run to the babies' room, pick them both up, and, holding one on each arm, wave them around proudly like two hunting trophies. "You're mad," I would shout. "Watch out or you'll drop them!" He would look at me, pretend to lose his balance to scare me, and then hug them both, swaying back and forth while he sang a lullaby in Ladin.

We took another nursemaid for the baby girl. Marcello quickly learned to walk, and he ran back and forth in the garden. I soon felt like my old self, and three weeks after Dolly was born I was thinking about resuming my Thursday salon. Sandrin wasn't of the same mind. "Be careful not to tire yourself," he said. "Wait a little while. What can it hurt?"

"It can hurt that I've already lost too much time with these two kids . . . and besides I feel fine. Why should I stay holed up?"

But actually Sandro never objected for long. Not because "he wasn't good at holding his own with his wife," as old Levi said, but because he loved me. It was as simple as that.

The news of a move to Cairo came unexpectedly. I don't know if Giulio arranged it on purpose to be mean, but I was sure that among his intentions was also the desire to put some distance between that "too weird" daughter-in-law and Trieste. Sandrin didn't know how to tell me, and he waited, as I had two years before, to be alone with me in the shelter of darkness. We had gone to see *The Masked Ball*. I remember because that was probably the last time Sandro sat with me in the box. In the carriage, instead of taking the road along the sea, Sandrin wanted to go down by the canal. We had never taken that way, and I sensed he was nervous, but I decided not to say anything. He asked the coachman to stop along the canal at Ponte Rosso. It was deserted at that hour. The water was unnaturally dark, and our footsteps seemed to follow the rhythm of the lapping sounds. Sandrin stared at the water flowing in the canal, and then very quickly, without any more hesitation, he began to explain that the bank intended to send him to the Cairo branch. It was a good opportunity, he said. Even his Voghera cousin had gone there for four years at the beginning of his career, and he liked it fine, just ask Elsa, who had a baby in Cairo without any problem whatsoever! We would be in colonial environments and I would have no trouble adapting, given my curiosity for new things . . .

While he was talking nonstop, I was thinking. And the thoughts were racing in my head. I knew that if I said no we wouldn't go, that the decision was up to me. And even though I was a little unsure, I felt a growing excitement.

By now Sandro was quiet and waiting. I didn't want to give him the impression that it was an easy decision. I wanted to make him worry about it a little, but inside I was already trembling with impatience: "If that's what your father wants . . ."

Sandro left a few months before we did to get everything ready. Then, one fine day, a cablegram arrived saying we could join him. The house was ready and we should bring with us two nurse-maids for the children and two housemaids. I couldn't think about anything else. There were so many things to organize! To start with, I had to order, for each family member, a wardrobe suitable for that climate so different from ours. Elsa Voghera gave me much valuable information in this regard and wrote a detailed list of all the indispensable things we wouldn't find in Egypt. I spent days preparing for the trip: I shopped, had things put away, wrote to Sandro asking for advice, read books about ancient history, and became more and more excited. The cruise, in addition, promised to be wonderful, also because many acquaintances would be on board, such as the Coens from Venice, who were friends of my sister Eugenia. We set sail on the twenty-seventh of June 1902 — not that I remember the date, but I kept the ticket. I can still see us arriving in the Alexandria port late one morning; the sun was so strong it made the parasol useless for protection. Facing me, a whitish expanse of houses and dust. Dust in the air, dust everywhere, or maybe it was sand, I don't know, but whatever it was, it was suffocating.

There was such confusion on shore that I was afraid I wouldn't find Sandrin, and even afraid I might lose the children, who were howling in the nursemaids' arms. I had sent the housemaids to get the luggage and waited there in that hell, alone, amid half-nude porters dashing around and shouting in that strange harsh language. I felt lost, unable to make up my mind what to do, until there appeared a very agitated Sandrin who was searching the crowd without seeing us. In order to make him hear me in that horrible *mismas*, I started yelling like a mussel vendor. Then Sandrin turned and began running toward me. He ran like a madman, elbowing his way through, and he hugged me so tightly I thought I might faint. "Where are the children?" he asked, looking around. And where should they be? In the shade with the nurses. Those poor creatures can't be left in the sun! I couldn't even finish before he ran over to take them both in his arms.

The heat was unbearable and I was exhausted. I tried covering my mouth with a handkerchief, but the dust penetrated everywhere. I grabbed Sandro's arm and begged him to take us away from there, to a quiet place.

Sandro had decided we should spend one night in Alexandria before facing the trip to Cairo. The hotel was a short distance away, on a pretty tree-lined street along the sea.

As soon as we got there I felt better. I sent the nurses to the rooms with the children and sat in the lobby to recover a bit. It was such an unusual setting, elegant and refined, full of curious characters: mostly French and English, some Arabs and very few women. The Boer war had just ended and we were surrounded by wounded or convalescent soldiers waiting to return to London, and then Indians, Persians, and Turks . . . Sandro bombarded me with questions, but my mind was on our trunks. I hadn't seen them since we arrived at the port and was beginning to worry. Besides, I had a headache and his suffocating concern was getting on my nerves.

Sandrin watched me, trying to guess my thoughts. Obviously he was worried I might be cross. I was tired, and wanted to make him pay a little; I wanted him to feel what I had been willing to give up to please him.

Poor dear, he was waiting for at least one word, one comment from me, and instead, nothing. Perhaps I overdid it, because he really didn't deserve it. I sat in silence for a long time, finished drinking the tea, leaned back on the cushions, and, with a big sigh that could have been of relief or of weariness, said: "Did you see how happy the children were to see you?"

The road to Cairo was in such poor condition that I thought we might never get there. However, the beautiful house compensated for the nightmare trip: two floors, colonial style, surrounded by an extensive palm grove. It seemed like an illustration for a Loti novel.

As far as comfort, it was not the greatest: water came from a well, the electricity was nothing to speak of, but that was what I had expected. We weren't in London, after all . . .

The rooms on the upper floor were spacious, blinding white, furnished with our things and objects new to me. How much work Sandrin had put into it, and how ill at ease and anxious he was while he waited for my verdict! This time I decided to give him the confirmation of my satisfaction immediately:

"You have done a wonderful job. Everything seems perfect."

To tell the truth, there was still a lot to do. First of all, to organize the house for entertaining: the party, as the English say. But that was my specialty, and I must say it didn't worry me. I had put together a nice squad of lively, quick young Arab women who knew *les lois de l'hospitalité* even better than I. To decorate the drawing room, I was inspired by paintings of some *orientalistes* that I liked so much. As for the table, I unearthed two marvelous French cooks able to add to their traditional gastronomy that pinch of exoticism that shouldn't be missing in such a background.

We were often invited to the home of Evelyn Bayring, the eccentric consul whom the Cairo residents called "The Lord" from the time he was elected baronet. An odd character, he had lived in India many years, knew a dozen languages and dialects, and lost his temper only when he heard talk of independence.

At his residence we also often encountered the khedive, King Abbas II Hilmi, whose presence bewitched me. There was something about that man that made me feel tremendously awkward, to the point that my friends teased I was in love. How ridiculous! It's just that he emanated a nobility and magnetism that had nothing to do with his prestigious title: the energy that sprang from his every movement never failed to attract everyone's attention. I watched him spellbound, and I suspect Sandrin was a little jealous, which was nonsense. How could he think that the king of Egypt would even deign to look at me? At Bayring's, though, there were also many boring Englishmen. When they started talking about hunting, horses, and croquet, I would go find some Boer war veteran and listen to his adventures with relief. The women were almost all drab and uninteresting to talk to, with the exception of two or three unusual personalities like Emma Scott-Williams, wife of a lawyer with the Suez Canal Company. She was the first to speak to me about Pankhurst, one of the suffragettes who fought for the women's right to vote in England. I was curious to hear what she had to say, even though, to tell the truth, that polemic had always seemed rather pointless to me. Why should we vote, if it's really only men who govern in any case?

❖

But there were not only the English in Cairo. There was also a considerable French community, so that at the Suez Company receptions we often found ourselves having to speak more than one language.

Sandrin always seemed proud to be able to show off a wife who could pass so easily from French to English, from Tuscan to German. Taking command of his baseless jealousy, he even bet King Abbas that within two or three months I would be able to converse with him "in his marvelous language." Flattered, I denied it.

We returned to Trieste at the end of 1904. I remember it well, because shortly afterward was the Yom Kippur ceremony at the temple, and Grandmother Volumnia made my ears ring with her scolding: "Look, now you've got to forget the king and all that nonsense. We aren't the least bit noble or royal. Our life isn't so easy. And don't get a big head, because how could poor Sandrin keep up with you?" All things considered, I was really fond of that woman. Her ignorance moved and amused me. It's not her fault, I thought, she was brought up that way, and what can the poor thing know about life? Luckily, the shofar had already sounded so I didn't have to answer her, and instead I hurried her along: Giulio and Sandro were waiting for everyone to gather under the tallith to receive the benediction.

Even though I had been unwilling to leave Cairo, I must admit that the period following our return to Trieste was so busy it soon canceled every regret. Sandrin worked long hours and was often too tired to join me. On the other hand, he never complained if he didn't find me home evenings. He knew very well that a woman of my social position had to respect a whole string of events and he was proud to see how much his wife was in demand. He enjoyed following news items in the society section about the receptions, the charities organized by our associations, or the accounts of first nights at the Teatro Comunale. When we were able to spend a little time together, we sat by the fireplace and commented on the journalists' silly observations. The only thing he disapproved of was my passion for cards. It's not nice, he said, for a lady to gamble, and I pretended not to know that what really annoyed him was my losses.

The evening that Marcello had his first attack of fever, I was at La Scala with some acquaintances. When I got home I found the house in a great turmoil. It was very late by then, and I was alarmed to see Dolly still up. She was crying on the sofa at the entrance hall, and the nanny explained that it had been impossible to persuade her to go to her room. She was trembling with fright.

Sandro had called the doctor, who was with him in Marcello's room. He stood by the bed and stroked his forehead. A forehead drenched, like the sheets. And as soon as I went in I knew I wouldn't make it.

I leaned against the door, inert. The light in the room was dim, but I heard the wheezing, the moans, and in the semidarkness I could see those wet curls, as if he had just come out of the sea . . .

I didn't stay long, but went to lie down in my room and wait.

For a long time.

Sandrin came into the room when I was half asleep, around dawn. He didn't say anything. He took off his jacket, stretched out on the bed beside me, and took my hand. For a while I pretended to be asleep; then, without opening my eyes, I murmured: "Don't ask anything of me, Sandro, because I can't cope with it." He didn't move. He squeezed my hand harder and then let go. I heard his breathing. I don't know if he was looking at me or not. He sat up on the edge of the bed, with his back to me, I believe, because his voice sounded far away: "Tomorrow I'll have the results of the laboratory analysis." That was all he said. I turned toward the window, watching the light that was beginning to filter in, and I stayed that way for a while, incapable of reacting. When I reached for his hand, he had already gone.

Over the following weeks, Sandrin was with Marcello so much it almost seemed like I didn't exist for him. He didn't try to stop me from going out; he never made a comment. And his indifference made me feel more and more useless.

And so the mechanism was set in motion that would finally destroy everything. He never asked anything of me, but others accused me of being cowardly, of running away, while Sandro took on the aura of a saint. And no one could get it into his head that that was precisely the point. Because I was so sure that *he* would make up for and forgive my every failing. He seemed to be encouraging me not to exert myself and to remain passive. How could I find any inner resources when I saw that he accepted all my defects?

With Sandro I felt ashamed, the shame you feel when you know you've made a mistake and it's too late to do anything. It's not at all easy to live with someone who constantly reminds you of a humiliating period of your existence.

He had a bed put in Marcello's room, and it was a relief for me to know he wouldn't be sleeping next to me. He wouldn't be doing that for a long time.

After we returned to Trieste we took up our former life, even knowing full well that nothing would ever be as it was before. We were each disappointed in turn, and as much as we tried to hide it, that disappointment would follow us forever.

The Triestines considered a stroll down Liston a sort of afternoon obligation, and that was precisely why Sandro invented any excuse he could to avoid it. On the rare times I asked him to accompany me he would mask his unwillingness behind a presumed inability to be with large groups. Actually Sandro was not at all the timid person he wanted to make out. He loved to be the center of attention, and if politics were being discussed, he could go on for hours. I, on the contrary, always wanted to be surrounded by people, and then, more often than not, I would get bored and couldn't wait to go somewhere else.

Liston went from the Corso to Piazza Grande. The walk was

studded with shops, cafés, wide areas where people could stop and talk of this and that, look at what the others were wearing, and comment about the last performance at the Teatro Comunale. I liked the ease with which one could move casually from one person to another, leave with an excuse, and then join up with the next acquaintance on the walk. It was much better than visiting in drawing rooms, where for some time I felt as though caught in a trap.

The rare times that Sandro accompanied me, he did it only to make me happy. And it's not comfortable for a woman to feel just the physical presence of the man beside her. I don't know where his mind was at those times. Certainly not with me.

I decided that Paris would be our salvation.

I got ready for that umpteenth life change with the same enthusiasm that I faced moving to Egypt, convinced that a little novelty was exactly what it took to spark our conjugal life.

I did everything I could to humor him, but Sandro didn't laugh at my jokes anymore and often acted worried, nervous, and impatient. And I got the impression I annoyed him merely by my presence, my way of being. If a word of dialect slipped out, if I came home with some new purchases, if I stopped in the street to talk with a friend, I could read great aggravation on his face for what I was, what I had always been, and what now, for some reason, he could no longer bear. He had also begun to pester me about money. He who had never refused me anything now began to control my expenditures. He wanted me to account for every single bill, in a manner that was irritating, to say the least.

In Paris the apartment on Rue Récamier was lovely, large, luminous. The children had two excellent tutors and Sandrin seemed satisfied with his new work.

Salons were now considered a little provincial in the French capital, but I didn't care. I had always liked receiving and I continued doing it, even at the cost of seeming *démodé* in the

Parisians' eyes. Sandrin, as always, let me go my own way, because as a matter of fact the children were all that was important to him. After Marcello's illness, he seemed obsessed by the fear of losing them, and he had it in his head to devote every moment of his free time to his children.

On Wednesdays, which were my reception days, I begged Sandro to make an effort. If I had to resign myself to his inexplicable refusal to invite his work colleagues, I didn't want to do without his presence. In order to persuade him, I resorted to any kind of argument:

"How can I be taken seriously in this town if you are never here? Did you know that many people think I'm a poor widow?"

Sometimes I even wormed a smile out of him.

According to him the current political controversies were the principal reason for his reluctance to be with certain French bourgeois, but I was convinced it was his poor knowledge of the language that created a problem for him.

The fact is that at every reception Sandrin systematically disappeared after less than an hour to shut himself up in the *"chambre de mademoiselle."*

It was actually time and not Paris that helped me to win him back. As the memory of the bad period with Marcello gradually faded, Sandro drew closer. Every once in a while his eyes lit up, he gave me more attention, and those little changes gave me hope. If I saw him dark, scowling, put out by some observation I made about Marcello's behavior, I apologized. I felt I had to "redeem" myself in his eyes, and even if I didn't consider it right, I had decided to sacrifice a little pride in order to get Sandro to renew his faith in me.

Dora, who had come to see me in Paris, had noticed at once how Sandro's manner toward me had changed, and all the time she was in Paris she badgered me with advice. According to her the best solution was "to give him another little one, then you'll see how everything is rekindled. It always works, believe me, and stop complaining, because after all it all depends on you."

I really didn't want another child, but I had to do something, and in the end I was convinced that it was worth the trouble to try.

My pregnancy was a surprise to everyone except me. Even Sandro had difficulty believing it. Certainly, I had done everything to revive our intimacy, but with all those quarrels over Marcello the moments of truce had become more and more infrequent. At least until Titti came along.

For Titti's birth was like a gust of the bora that swept away every misunderstanding and worry for a while.

I even stopped going out evenings, now convinced I was the only one capable of putting the baby to sleep, and I teased Sandro that he was jealous: "I'm stealing your job," I told him laughingly, and both of us ended up going to my Nacci's room to sing him songs, rock him, and tell him stories. And while I held that baby in my arms, Sandro looked at me with the love of long ago.

With Marcello, however, the peace was never destined to last, and as much as I tried to fool myself, I soon had to take this reality into account.

What had wounded me most about the Freud business was Sandrin's condescending attitude. He was sure that I wanted to go to Vienna just to be fashionable. He couldn't understand that I was really interested in that new science; to him it was merely a whim, a childish impulse.

I was offended by his lack of faith, but it didn't discourage me — perhaps because in my heart I had decided to attribute it to a fit of pique rather than to lack of respect.

After that trip, however, Sandro did everything to make it obvious he had taken the situation in hand: we were to leave Paris, return to Trieste, and then escape to Italy. He, the head of the family, would make the decisions, and he seemed absolutely determined not to allow me any say.

❖

It seemed to me that to abandon everything in order to take refuge in Italy was insane, and I tried every means to talk Sandro into giving up his plan. In Trieste we had a house, family, friends . . . what did those ridiculous stories about the fatherland have to do with us?

"You don't know what you're talking about . . . ," he replied drily.

"Oh, yes I do. Where do you want us to go? Do you want us to do like Mason Mayer who took to his heels and let the Austrians steal everything? And what do we do with the children? And the bank and our business interests?"

"For heaven's sake, when did you ever care about our business interests?"

Sandrin shut himself up for hours and hours with old Riefenstal, the bank's accountant, trying to arrange it so the Austrians couldn't seize everything after we left, which was exactly what happened.

Three weeks before Sonnino signed the London Treaty we were already in Venice. Then in Livorno, Florence, and God only knows where else. For the first year we made the rounds of the family. While he looked for a place to settle in Italy, Sandro haggled with the Austrian administration in an attempt to save what was possible to save, and he sent medical certificates to justify his presence on Italian territory. When I think about it — what a waste of energy . . .

The children were at risk: I decided to send Dolly to boarding school, Titti went on haphazardly with a number of tutors, and Marcello . . . I've already said enough about him.

After a time we moved to a very beautiful villa in the middle of Genoa, and I could finally take out of storage the few pieces of furniture we brought from Trieste.

Sandro seemed feverish, always dashing here and there. He would return to Genoa several times a month, and each time he would anxiously question me about our situation: "Is everything all right? Are you happy with the arrangement? Do you want a different maid?" His questions and behavior were frenzied. Then he would hole up in the study with his paperwork. He was so involved with his business that even when things came to a head with Marcello he continued to act as though it had nothing to do with him. How could he, the one who would sell his soul for his children, suddenly not care about anything or anyone? For him there was nothing but business, just business.

Only later did I learn about the ugly rumors going around about Castaldi and me at the sanatorium. Just imagine if I would have stayed so long! Sandrin wrote me from Genoa that the war was drawing to a close, that soon we would be able to return to Trieste. He asked for news of Marcello: the cure had been going on for eight months and perhaps that was enough. And had that Augusto Castaldi, whom he knew I had met, been some help?

I had no inkling of the pain behind those words. At another time I might have been suspicious, and then I certainly would have done everything possible not to make the situation worse. But the Sandrin I knew would never let himself be taken in by all that gossip. As far as I could tell his anxiety was tied exclusively to the hospitalization expense.

I felt very agitated when we returned home. The disastrous result of Marcello's treatment was obvious to everyone and Sandro couldn't keep from demanding an explanation.

During supper no one had the courage to face the subject, and I remember that Dolly left right after dessert, to leave us alone.

While filling his pipe, Sandro spilled a handful of tobacco and stooped over to pick it up.

He was a little stiff, like an old man: his back reminded me very much of his father.

"Let it be. I'll call Angelina," I told him.

He circled the dining room restlessly. He seemed to have decided not to launch any accusations, but I followed him with nerves tensed, ready to defend myself.

"Maybe he needs more love," he declared point blank.

"Are you talking about me?"

"Not only, Gemma, not only."

I wasn't at all pleased with the turn the conversation was taking. I was afraid Sandro would force me to say something about Castaldi. And I had no intention of justifying myself for a nonexistent fault.

There was a long silence, interrupted only by Sandro's puffing on his pipe to relight it. Then he turned toward me and murmured, without acrimony, wearily: "There are people who manage to bring out the worst in those around them. They don't do it on purpose. It's stronger than they are . . ."

Was he referring to himself or to Marcello?

Naturally the villa in Trieste was confiscated. The best furniture had been saved by the old Levis, who moved it to their house before the war broke out. The remainder, except for the few things we had taken to Genoa, went up in smoke.

I found Dolly very changed, and it was obvious she hadn't missed me a bit!

Titti had grown. He was becoming a little man, but his face had lost none of its sweetness.

When I learned of Dolly's engagement, I was a little puzzled. It wasn't like Sandro to put before me a *fait accompli* on questions of this nature. In fact, that was the kind of business he usually wanted nothing to do with. I couldn't understand the hurry or the guilty look I saw in my husband's eyes. When I tried to find out more about it he would give a reply absentmindedly, muttering that the marriage was an excellent solution. A solution for what? I asked myself.

Anyone who has not experienced a war cannot imagine the joy, the sense of freedom that explodes when it is over. It's like recovering from a long illness that everyone considered incurable. One thinks only of life. At least one should. But at our house death was everywhere. Grim faces, the smell of stale smoke, silence. I couldn't take it anymore, and too bad for Marcello, because I had already done too much for him. Too bad for Dolly, whose future was decided. Too bad for Sandro, because he certainly couldn't blame me if we had lost nearly everything.

Titti was the only one I cared for, the only one I wanted to save from that ruin.

I couldn't wait to move back to Genoa, to the only house still ours, surrounded by my furniture. I couldn't stand those rented quarters close by the Levis' villa. I would come back home late and find Sandro in the library alone, immersed in some book that perhaps he was only pretending to read in order to give me the impression he hadn't been waiting up for me.

He wanted to make me feel guilty, and as usual he didn't ask me anything in an attempt to show how understanding and willing to forgive he was. At least that was what I thought. But after what happened perhaps I should find the courage to confess to myself that I didn't understand anything about my husband at that time.

His attitude goaded me into provoking him: at a certain point he will have to rebel, I thought. It was just another challenge. I expected him to stop me. Who could have imagined that he would be the one to stop?

When Sandrin came up with the idea of giving a dinner for the family of Dolly's fiancé, I knew at once he had something up his sleeve. There was a light in his eyes that I hadn't seen for a long time, and I thought he had decided to make a surprise announcement about the marriage date. I didn't understand what the devil Castaldi had to do with it, but I thought that if my husband believed he would embarrass me he was badly mistaken.

I don't know what meaning Sandrin wanted to give to his death. It is commonly said that death has no meaning, but a suicide . . . Well, it has to have one.

Perhaps he wanted to give me my freedom and chose the most painful way to do it.

The note he left in his study was a lot like him: generous, altruistic, a real burden for someone who has something to reproach herself for.

Months later, leafing through my old notebook, I found these words on the last page:

I loved you, I love you, and I will always love you.

Sandrin

Who knows when he wrote them.

TITTI

*I*T'S DIFFICULT TO speak about someone you haven't had time to know . . .

Difficult to understand how much to attribute to memory and how much to stories heard over the years. Images of childhood are mixed with faded photographs, and in my mind's eye even his face seems immobile, as though posed.

I don't remember his voice, only a sort of music in the distance. How did he walk, how did he bend his head as he lit his pipe, how did his face light up when he smiled?

If I delve into my memories, I find a face next to mine, a slender, long hand that caresses my head, looking into my eyes; a nursery rhyme in Ladin, obsessive, sweet, that I loved so much and that he sang to me every evening. I still remember the music, but I've forgotten the words.

I called him "Babbo" sometimes to honor the Tuscan, the language of the heart, the one we were proud of.

He had an enormous black mustache that I loved to turn up, curling it over my fingers to make him look like a character from *A Thousand and One Nights*. And that makes me think he must have often carried me in his arms, a rare thing for a man of those times. Yes, I remember his embrace, the swing of his hips when he picked me up, his sweet and triumphant look when he gazed at me.

My father liked children. That's what everyone always said, including Mama, who often recalls: "Your father loved the company of children more than adults."
I like this peculiarity of his. It helps me imagine his inner world, which of course will remain forever unknown.

My first real memories, the clearest, are of 1916, on the beach at Arenzano where our family spent the summers during the war. He would join us once in a while on Sundays. He never wore a bathing suit. He was always dressed in black, shoeless, with his pant legs rolled up. Mama would fuss at him, saying that he would ruin his suit, but he paid no attention to her protests and laughed at seeing her so worked up. When he came with us to the sea he generally sat in the shade; he would light his pipe and look around as he smoked. Then he would start leafing through the newspaper without concern about the wind or sand. As soon as I saw him I would run up and sit on the ground next to his lounge chair. I didn't know my father well. The war broke out six years after I was born, and the precarious position we found ourselves in didn't allow us to be together often. And because I didn't know him well I felt endless admiration for him. I didn't know what he did and I imagined him in the strangest situations, sure that he was a spy infiltrated in the Austrian troops who returned to Italy every once in a while to make his secret reports. I questioned him often about life in the trenches and on the front, and he looked at me in amazement, saying he had never been there, that he was not a soldier. But I knew he was lying to protect his double life.

To tell the truth, it was Marcello who put those espionage stories in my head: he really enjoyed telling me about Papa's wonderful adventures, and I believed every word.

When I accidentally found out, from something Dolly said, that Marcello had invented everything, I cried one whole night. Not so much because of the deceit as out of disappointment: the discovery of really having an ordinary father like all the others, who went to an office every day with a briefcase stuffed with paperwork.

My close relationship with Marcello was an unfathomable mystery to Papa, something he felt duty-bound to protect me from. He often interrupted our little meetings in my brother's room to ask me to go with him with any pretext whatever. I obeyed, but I knew he really had nothing to say to me. He only wanted me to get out of that closed, smoke-filled room. It was obvious Sandro was afraid of Marcello, which I didn't understand at all.

When we were alone at the end of the war — Papa, Dolly, and I — I felt a little off base for a few weeks. I missed Marcello's irony, his games. I missed Mama's enthusiasm. I had never been alone in the house with my father, and I was afraid of being bored, of not finding a way to fill my days. Instead, an unusual atmosphere was created, as if suddenly a lid was lifted, a dike broken. And so I got to know my father and my sister, whom I loved of course, but who always made me a little uneasy, perhaps because she was so serious and little inclined to let go.

What a strange time that was. Shunted from one city to another, with the family separated for reasons that had nothing to do with the war, we managed in our own way to create a nucleus, however unorthodox. My father and Dolly formed a real couple, more than my parents were. Dolly ran the house wonderfully, working real miracles in getting food and other necessities. Although I was still a child, I realized that an unaccustomed serenity reigned around me, and that calm soon made me forget the anxiety I felt at being separated from my mother for the first time.

I enjoyed hiding in a corner of the parlor to listen to Sandro and Dolly comment on newspaper articles in the evening. Their discussions were very animated and they often disagreed. I kept quiet while listening to their incomprehensible exchanges. When they noticed my presence they would both suddenly stop in midsentence in order, I believe, not to offend my young ears with the summary of violent events going on around us.

The situation was so chaotic that the presence of a nanny or a tutor had become impractical. Therefore my studies were guided in part by my sister, who was in charge of literature, poetry, and geography, and in part by my father, who taught me history, mathematics, and Hebrew. It was such fun with Dolly because she concentrated exclusively on authors she loved the most, happily ignoring the classics in order to spend hours on the great Romantic novels. With my father, on the other hand, there was no way to slide by. He had his own way of talking about history, making it seem like a very long fable whose adventures were all connected. His recitations were so passionate that he made even the most insignificant details come alive, and more than once I was surprised to imagine with open eyes a dinner in ancient Egypt or a conversation with Charlemagne.

Strange to say, but I believe I learned much more during that period than I ever did later, and even today the little I know about history or poetry I owe to those improvised lessons.

The war over, as we got ready for what we believed would be our decisive return to Trieste, Dolly very courageously took the situation in hand. Gemma's letters from the sanatorium didn't reveal when she might be able to join us, and it made me so sad that it seemed natural to conclude that my father's sudden melancholy was due to that uncertainty also.

In Trieste, Father took up that serious manner I had always known, but after all I was used to it and gave it no particular importance. However, the return of his melancholy didn't make him forget his fatherly duties, which he expressed in such different ways with each of us. My sister had become his fixed companion at the dinners and meetings that kept him occupied three or four times a week. I would watch them leave together. She, proud to be on her father's arm; he, proud of his daughter's dark beauty.

With me, however, Papa got it into his head to have me visit a different part of Trieste every day. He really loved his city and couldn't bear for one of his children not to know every corner perfectly. The Rive, Miramare, the narrow streets of Borgo Theresian were our daily goals, punctuated by regular pauses in front of favorite cafés and pastry shops — almost always closed due to the war — where Papa would describe the specialty of each in great detail. We went to the citrus warehouses on Via Torrebianca, where on the eve of Sukkoth the market swarmed with Greek tradesmen selling fruit for the holiday to Jewish merchants come from the eastern Diaspora. I was enchanted with those colors, and that mix of unknown and exotic tongues. I didn't understand the excitement of certain groups of Russians and Poles, so strange with those tangled locks of hair and odd Hasidic headgear trimmed in fur . . .

"You mustn't laugh at them."

"But they're so funny."

"If you were one of them you would find us funny."

"But there are more of us."

"Being in the majority doesn't mean you're right."

Often the customers argued loudly in Yiddish with the sellers, and then Father explained that the tension was over the staggering price increases with the approaching holiday. The bitter smell of citrus fruit, its brilliant yellow, the huge crates carried from one end of the warehouse to the other, the outlandish clothes, the money passing from hand to hand . . .

Sandro would occasionally pick up a piece of fruit and smell it, looking at me out the corner of his eye with a conspiratorial air; then he enjoyed launching into a long conversation with a Greek or someone from Corfu standing close by. I was amazed and happy to watch him: not only was I discovering a new world, but I was also learning to understand my father.

❖

In spite of all Sandro's efforts to keep me busy, I missed Mama so intensely that I was unable to hide my anguish and more than once broke into sobs in front of Papa, shaming myself for behaving so childishly. I would have liked to be more courageous! For him, in order not to make him suffer, but I couldn't control myself and every time I felt the tears begin to roll down my cheeks I tried to hide, because I knew that he would barely be able to contain his own . . .

One fine day Sandro came home with a round basket tied with a large white silk ribbon. Papa knew that one of my greatest joys was unwrapping surprises. I tore off the ribbon, anxious to discover what was inside. He couldn't have given me a nicer gift: in the basket was a puppy of my favorite breed, a spotted pointer whom I called Picchio.

Picchio and I were inseparable and, as might be expected, his presence in the house changed our family routine. The ritual of walking him was established, which from time to time Dolly or Father had to take over. I don't think it thrilled them very much, especially Dolly, who had never been an animal lover. But they would have done anything to see me smile and I, I must admit, didn't hesitate to take advantage of the situation.

Then I remember the big news of the engagement. Big for me, who gave poor Dolly no peace by excitedly peppering her with questions, unconsciously showing no mercy to her wounded spirit. As far as I was concerned the engagement should be nothing but a joyous occasion, and I wanted to experience every bit of that happiness. Besides, I liked the so-called Brazilian a lot. Every time he came over, he brought me candied fruit or licorice sticks and from that I deduced that he had to be a good person and that my sister was really a lucky woman.

Finally Mama returned.

And with her, Marcello.

It took awhile to reestablish contact. I had almost forgotten how his sick body looked, and for the first time I felt uneasy in his presence. Yes, in a certain sense I had grown away from him and it made me feel guilty, because I knew how important it was for my brother to recapture the special bond that had always been between us.

As for Mama, she was exactly what she was before: radiant, happy, and even more beautiful than I remembered. She smothered me with kisses, hugging me so tightly I had to ask her laughingly more than once to loosen her grip a bit. She had missed me, that was obvious. Almost as much as I had missed her . . .

That evening I went into the garden to look for Picchio. I looked under the hawthorn bush where he usually hid to tease me. Sandro and Marcello were sitting on a stone bench under the cedar of Lebanon. They didn't know I was there and I didn't make a sound — not that I wanted to spy on them, but I knew it annoyed them to see me worry about the dog too much. Therefore I decided to continue my search quietly, but it was suddenly interrupted by a kind of strangled yell. It was Marcello's sharp cry when he got overwrought, but I couldn't understand what he and Father were talking about that could have triggered such agitation. I stayed crouched down behind the bush, more out of fear than curiosity, and finally I understood that the reason for the crisis was Dolly's engagement. Marcello said some terrible things, and in his excitement he provoked the usual dyspnea that suffocated him. Sandro listened to him in silence. I couldn't see him, but I imagined him sitting next to his son with his head bent . . . Marcello accused our father of not having the slightest consideration for Dolly's feelings, of promising her to the first wealthy suitor who came along just because he was incapable of curbing his wife's "insatiable appetites." When Marcello was through venting his feelings, Sandro sighed sadly. His voice was trembling and I could barely hear: "You always think you see the whole picture; you think you know everything. But, my poor son, you don't know anything. You are the avenging angel, judging from the height of your wisdom . . . But sooner or later the judge is mistaken, and believe me I wouldn't want to be in your shoes when you have to come to terms with your intransigence." He stood up clearing his throat in an attempt to recover his normal tone of voice, and before going away, he wearily, impassively, added: "Anyway, think whatever you want. It makes no difference to me at this point."

There was a long silence. A silence so absolute that I was frightened Marcello would discover me. Then, after a few moments, I heard a kind of weak, imperceptible lament that gradually became a single horrible gasp. Marcello had burst into tears, and as always happened when he was gripped by emotion, he was having one of those terrible and lengthy crises of breathlessness.

I ran to the house to call the nurse.

Of our stay in Trieste, I remember mainly the walks with Papa and Marcello, so different in their chosen goals, but actually very similar.

Naturally I was unaware of much that was going on in the house, and I really wasn't very concerned. Mama came and went like a madwoman while Father stayed holed up in his office until late in the evening. At Genoa things only got worse. Now Papa never left his study, always absorbed in complicated financial accounts. That was something absolutely novel for me. I wasn't used to seeing him in the house during the day, and for a while I thought he had decided to change his routine in order to keep a closer watch on Marcello.

Now and then he would call me from behind the closed door. How profound his melancholy must have been to make him want to go on walks with Picchio and me so often! During those long walks in the park of Villa delle Rose (we never left the garden because Father had a terrible fear of the few automobiles that had begun to circulate on the city streets), he spoke very little. He asked questions about my lessons with the tutor, spoke one or two sentences in Hebrew to see if I was able to respond . . . At times he asked me for news of my brother and sister, as if he never had the opportunity to see them. I answered without thinking, telling him reassuring and positive things. As far as I could tell, because I had never been a keen observer, the overall situation was the same as ever. He pretended to be reassured, but I sensed in his questions an underlying feeling of inadequacy that kept him from being really at peace.

He was stepping aside, almost as if he felt he was in the way . . .

On that day I am sure I heard him come very early into my room. Mama says I imagined everything because of the emotional strain, but I know it wasn't like that. It's too vivid a memory to be just the fruit of my imagination. He came in my room before dawn and stood silently in the threshold for a time. He didn't say anything and I pretended to be asleep. I could feel his look fixed on me, an intense look, almost violent. There was such a strong tension in him that I could feel it flowing over me. And though I didn't open my eyes even for an instant, I know for certain that it was he, and that he stood there for a very long time . . .

On the evening of the fateful dinner, Mama had me put on my most elegant suit, the one that Uncle Riccardo had just brought me from London. From her excitement I understood that we had important guests and that it was a very special occasion.

Papa stayed in his study almost until the first guests arrived: Dolly's "fiancé" and his father. He greeted them extremely cordially, and in turn the two of them lavished me with compliments. Father asked Dolly to go get Marcello, who had not yet come out of his room. When it was almost time to sit down at the table the last guest arrived, the lawyer Castaldi. I probably hadn't seen the lawyer more than a couple of times, but I didn't like him because Marcello, who couldn't stand the fellow, talked very badly of him. The last image I have of my father is the gesture he made as he sat my mother at the table. His slight bow and outstretched right arm that opened gently in midair . . .

I've asked myself a thousand times why that gesture has stuck in my mind, as if there was a hidden meaning to it, as if it contained some secret message.

❖

I remember nothing of what happened afterward except for the echo of the shot, a distant echo, because I was already in bed.

An echo that took my childhood away with it.

I know about the note he left. Dolly told me many years later, and then I understood many things. Many things, but not everything. His death could have had many causes, too many. What had really made him do it? Shame over the bankruptcy? Pain over the presumed betrayal? A sense of powerlessness and defeat? What was the last straw that made him take the final step? What was he thinking that morning when he came to my room?

And if I had not pretended to be sleeping, if I had talked to him, if I had called to him and held him close and asked him to sing me a lullaby in Ladin?

CASTALDI

DOLLY

*A*s hard as I try it is very difficult to find anything to say about that man. Pathetic provincial notable, self-important, culturally limited to the three things learned by heart and systematically served up on the least occasion to impress his audience. It almost seems like a waste of time to speak of him. Augusto Castaldi was the prototype parvenu of the epoch, a man without talent but capable of making his way in the best society with *bons mots* and flippant gallantries. Short, bald, with that ridiculous and useless monocle stuck to his right eye, always dressed in a dark double-breasted jacket too tight at the waist, not to mention his garish two-toned patent-leather shoes. He seemed like a Mussolini caricature, a resemblance ahead of its time that, on the other hand, he encouraged as much as possible after the advent of fascism . . .

Castaldi met Mama in the sanatorium, where he was undergoing detoxification for opium, although that was not the official reason for his presence. He was somehow acquainted with one of Father's relatives — more of a business relationship, I believe, than a friendship. Other than that there is little I can say about him; I left home as soon as he set foot in it. After Father's death I had one objective: to get away. I had to get free of his constant intrusions: wherever I was, whatever I was doing, Papa slipped into my thoughts. He seemed to be there at the most unexpected moments and I did everything to get him out of my mind, to remove the image of his face. I didn't think that running away would make me free, but at least we would be alone, he and I. And perhaps if I found myself alone with his memory I would begin to understand.

I didn't want to hear any more about Gemma or the supposed engagement or the financial difficulties. They were no longer part of my life. The last chain binding me to my family was broken and all that was left was escape if I wanted to avoid their fate. I went to visit a cousin in Turin for a while before going to Davos, where I became the companion of a friend afflicted with tuberculosis of the bone. This was my decision and no one could make me change my mind. To tell the truth, no one tried to, certainly not Mama who couldn't wait to be free of me. But even Marcello didn't try to stop me. He understood that this was the only way for me to save myself, to find myself again, to escape the oppressive weight of what had happened. For him it was already too late, and I didn't even try to convince him to follow me. His course was plotted; it was only a question of time . . . And so I left without a care about the Brazilian, my mother's lover, the little bit of money I could expect and that clearly would never arrive. Nothing was important anymore, and for the first time I was thinking only about myself, without worrying about what would become of Marcello and Titti.

Mama married Castaldi just one year after Father's death. The ceremony was private and discreet, taking place in Venice. We were all there, but I left right after the courthouse wedding.

I had to see Castaldi each summer, however, because the family went to the sea at Marina di Pisa, where Augusto's parents had a splendid villa. If I wanted to spend a little time with my brothers and keep a minimal relationship with my mother I was forced to be his guest.

A real torment, except for hunting in the swamp, our only interest in common. Castaldi aroused feelings of hostility and contempt in me. He was so inferior in every way to my father, so crass and predictable, that just having to look at him was more than I could bear. And yet, I know that that poor fellow wasn't a bad man and his only fault, if you can call it a fault, was his inability to accept himself for what he was, to accept his petty nature even though it caused him unhappiness. Castaldi was sincerely, madly in love with my mother. He would have done anything for her, as he demonstrated, and it could be said that in reality he was just another victim of Gemma's selfishness, her last pawn.

In Pisa, Gemma's life fell into the frenetic rhythm that had always characterized it. As far as I know the couple mixed with the fascist notables, as well as the many community members enrolled in the party. Gemma ordered her wardrobes from Paris, complete with perfumes, accessories, and audacious hats, in which she sallied around the streets of that provincial town: excessive, out of keeping, totally inappropriate. Augusto, no less fascinated than she by novelty, fell in with every one of Gemma's whims, often adding unexpected and fantastic gifts. As though it were nothing, he was capable of driving up to the house in a brand-new automobile or with a *dernier cri* phonograph, not to mention the continual stream of gifts for Titti, who could have opened up shop with all the bicycles, guns, and English stamps.

He treated my brothers with embarrassing consideration. His every gesture was determinedly kind, and his persistent attempts to conquer the by now totally apathetic Marcello were painful. At what point could Castaldi's pale and predictable nature and my brother's twisted and impenetrable character ever converge?

The tone Marcello used with his stepfather was so intolerably caustic that it even exasperated me. Not that Castaldi noticed it (he told everyone that Marcello had become docile and affectionate and that the change was due to his "positive influence on the boy"), but Marcello's behavior reminded me sadly of certain oppressive evenings only a few years ago, when my brother's pitiless attacks had Papa as their target.

❖

Marcello's torment, his agony, his cynical self-destruction were carried out right under Castaldi's gaze without his noticing it. I don't believe I have ever met anyone in my life more obtuse or more insensitive to human psychology, and this blindness was so much more surprising in a man whose personal vicissitudes should have given him some insight into Marcello's drama and what was about to happen. And yet I am still convinced that Augusto never really understood that Marcello's death was not that "unfortunate incident," which he bewailed in reference to "Gemma's misfortune."

After Marcello's demise, Castaldi's role in the family became more problematic. Mama played the part of the victim persecuted by destiny and poor Augusto, who had married her both as a form of social redemption and to spite his family, suddenly found himself with a woman ostracized from that very society he had mistakenly thought he had conquered through her. For Titti, totally defeated, now deprived of the protection that his brother's sharp critical sense had represented for him, Castaldi was transformed over the years into a sort of putative father. Under his influence, Titti was, like all the children of that epoch, a fervent follower of the fascist delirium, finally becoming a convinced Avanguardista.

It might seem strange that amid such tragedy and pain, the only truly unforgivable sin of that politically ignorant wretch, as far as I was concerned, was that he dragged the only brother left to me into this delirium. Seeing photos of Titti, a young and magnificent youth, in fez and black shirt brought tears to my eyes. And the memory of my mother's big to-do over his achievements arouses bursts of uncontrollable anger in me even today. Poor Titti, to have as a male model a self-important, insignificant, fascist bourgeois, the most horrifying prototype of what the Italy of that time could offer!

To escape the gossip and backbiting, Mama and Castaldi moved to Padua, where Augusto began collaborating with a rather prestigious law firm. From what I subsequently learned, however, the proceeds from his work were certainly not enough to satisfy his needs, seeing that Castaldi was constantly asking his parents for money, who desperately tried to do all they could to help him.

I very rarely went to Padua, a city I didn't care for, and which made me feel very sad and melancholy. My life was now elsewhere, but as hard as I tried to build a separate existence, I was not completely able to burn the bridges connecting me to my family. I don't know if it was my attachment to Titti or my residual and tormented sense of duty toward Mama that made me visit them a couple of times a year. The fact is, I deliberately submitted to that rite with great agonizing, given their circle of friends and acquaintances . . .

The war had changed the cards on the table, and just as it ruined some people, it allowed others to become wealthy. The world belonged to them now. Mama was able to switch from one to the other with apparent ease, even though I suspect she had some problem adapting. Castaldi was one of those who until a few years before would have done anything to be accepted by the *beau monde* and who could now do without it just as well. He was a commoner with a university education who had known how to take advantage of the postwar social upheaval. His sense of victory was obvious, and his wife was his most coveted trophy: he had succeeded in wrenching her from those phony gentlemen who now belonged to the past and who were presently forced to treat him, if not with respect, at least politely. Even Grandfather Giulio had to seek his help to meet the innumerable debts left by Father. As for Gemma, she took sides with the strongest, the new powerful, those who had the future of the country in hand, and her fascist faith entered the new order of things. The decadent aristocrats, the protagonists of a society that until a few years ago she had so wanted to dazzle, were now part of a way of life that had disappeared along with their wealth.

Titti often took part in military rallies and sent me exasperating postcards apprising me of Il Duce's merits. During my stays at the villa in Marina di Pisa, I tried to open his eyes, but it was a waste of time. Castaldi exuberantly proclaimed the patriotism and moral worth of Mussolini; he praised what he called "his rational and fateful vision of the economy," and he persisted in proudly showing me the map of "our wonderful colonial empire." That was the way Castaldi talked, always with pompous words and pat phrases, a probable consequence of his profession whose prose, of course, is drenched in high-flown rhetoric. Gemma was fascinated by it and commented in awe: "Listen to how well he speaks!" Poor Mama, she who was able to go from one language to another with ease, to flaunt Ladin or Triestine when required, suddenly appeared proud of the artificial Italian of an uncultured man. But if it was immediately obvious that Augusto served to indulge Gemma's narcissism, Mama also supplied an analogous function for him. You only had to watch how Castaldi strutted when he held the arm of that still awesomely beautiful woman! The extreme satisfaction, the feigned detachment with which he observed the other men to reassure himself that they were all struck by his wife's beauty, was perfectly counterbalanced by the coquettishness with which Gemma watched the "ladies" out the corner of her eye, all spellbound by the "virile attractiveness" of her husband. Yes, in this way they were truly a perfect couple and perfectly matched. But their equilibrium rested on a very fragile foundation flawed at the outset.

I received Titti's letter in Davos in March 1928. It was a confused, embarrassed letter that wandered in allusions rather than getting to the point. Between the lines, however, I understood what he was trying to tell me, and the news of Castaldi's relapse had a whiplash effect on me. That those two shared a totally irresponsible way of facing life was perfectly obvious. That they both loved to live above their means, to overdo things, to make an impression . . . But this was too much!

And yet no one knew better than I how they met, and the gossip about the real reason for the hospitalization of Augusto, notoriously enslaved to opium, had reached me almost at once.

But it is as if I had put all that out of my mind, and not out of naïveté, as some could reproach me, but out of pure and simple incredulity. I would never have imagined for a single instant that a human being could so persistently repeat the same mistakes; that he could almost obsessively go from one nightmare to another. It was inconceivable to me.

When I reached the villa it was already too late. Castaldi had been gone for three days. Titti didn't give himself a moment's peace. He couldn't understand how such an apparently strong man could hide such a weakness. It never crossed his mind that Mama could have worsened things by her ways of behaving, with her unhealthy ability to make believe it was nothing, pathetically and stubbornly continuing to play her part of the happy couple. At the same time it didn't cross my mind to confront her about it. I had given up trying to understand her destructive mechanisms, the tenacity with which she jumped headlong into the most perverse situations. I only wanted to find Castaldi — not so much for his own good, I must admit, as to put an end to the intolerable uncertainty. To find him, smooth the waters, and leave.

I never would have imagined that that poor little man, who didn't even know how to swim, would one day find the courage to jump off a bridge . . .

GEMMA

ERE GOES THE third one!" Dolly wrote beneath a beautiful photo portrait taken of Augusto and me in the park of Marina di Pisa the last summer we spent together. That cruel comment was not like her, but the death of her father and Marcello had unleashed some shockingly violent reactions in Dolly.

That evening at the gambling table, when Augusto approached me for the first time, I had been losing a considerable amount.

I remember his amused smile as he whispered in my ear, "You'd better change tables." At first I was irritated: who does that fellow think he is to give me advice when I've never seen him before in my life. Then I took a better look. Good heavens, what power! Very young, for heaven's sake, more or less Marcello's age, but something so strong, so protective emanated from him that had nothing to do with the years. He was a man, someone who made you feel secure.

And besides he was right. It absolutely was not my night. As soon as I stopped playing I sat down near the fireplace where some other guests were conversing. Of course, I was waiting for him to come talk to me — certainly nothing wrong with that! And Augusto was not the kind to keep me waiting long . . .

❖

That's how we became friends. It was a real miracle, because during that time Marcello's behavior didn't leave much room for social life. Augusto understood the situation immediately, and he also knew how to get around difficulties, finding it safer not even to say hello to me when I was with Marcello. But it wasn't a trivial strategy to ward off gossip, as many *petits esprits* have insinuated, only a matter of simple prudence: it took very little for Marcello to lose control, and we really didn't want to attract attention.

I believe everyone has had at some time the instinctive feeling of being able — apparently without reason — to trust someone completely. A kind of impulse that can inspire us almost against our better judgment to confide in a stranger things that we don't find easy to confess even to ourselves . . .

I had such faith in Augusto that when the doctors began to suggest that isolation was the only way to cure Marcello, I let him convince me it would be better to extend the normal cure, because terrible things were said about isolation, and until there was an alternative, he told me, it was better to avoid extreme remedies.

We took walks, talked, laughed. In that place of death and disease was it wrong to look for a little life?

More than three months went by without the slightest sign of improvement, but the doctors kept telling me "it's too early," "not yet," and Augusto also agreed that one must have patience with these things.

Then, suddenly, Marcello got it into his head that he was better, and since the war had been over for several months, it was time to go home. He didn't think it would be right for me to continue "to enjoy myself" using his illness as an excuse, because "even if Papa allows it, I don't want the burden of this responsibility; therefore, get our bags packed so we can leave here by the end of the week . . ."

For a long time I had given up listening to him, but he was right this once: we had to go home.

❖

Back in Trieste it took a little time before Augusto and I could see each other — certainly not because we considered it "improper," but many things had changed and it wasn't easy to put order in that kerfuffle. Our house was still sequestered, Dolly was engaged to a stranger, Marcello was by now completely out of his senses, and Sandro brooded from morning to night. To be honest, I didn't even think about Augusto at first. For me our friendship had merely been a lovely digression.

Our first meeting in Trieste took place on Liston, where I sometimes walked in the afternoon. Augusto was with Emilia Bruson, the wife of one of Sandro's colleagues, and they were walking side by side very naturally. I was a little cold with him, certainly not because of Emilia, but because I had learned that Augusto had often come to Trieste for work during that period, and the fact that he had never left me a note had annoyed me more than a little.

What a fast worker! In two minutes he had convinced me of his good faith, and a short time later I found myself with the two of them drinking a cup of hot chocolate at the Café degli Specchi.

With her usual tiresome insistence, Emilia was dying to hear how and where we met, and to save me from embarrassment, Augusto dusted off the story of a prewar dinner, of which I remembered little or nothing.

To make the story more credible he embroidered it with many imaginary details that would have made his interlocutor suspicious if she hadn't been so completely taken in by his patter: "Signora Levi was wearing a periwinkle dress" — Volumnia . . . in periwinkle! — "and had prepared one of those dishes . . . those typical dishes . . ." The idiot didn't know how to continue! For a few seconds I let him squirm. Then, in the face of his confusion I was suddenly struck by pity:

"*Gefilte fisch* . . ." I suggested with a wink.

"Exactly, exactly . . . it's a foreign word. That's why I didn't remember it . . . a real delicacy!"

❖

That was Augusto, always ready to play along, able to make me happy even at the worst of times, when I felt everything was collapsing around me.

We started seeing each other again — some walks along the sea, a chocolate together, and an occasional concert. Sometimes he went shopping with me, advising me about what to choose . . . nothing more. Augusto was becoming my entertainment companion, while Sandro continued to be my companion in bad luck.

All I know is that I could not have survived Sandrin's death if Augusto hadn't been there to help me. Of all my acquaintances, I can't remember one who gave me a hand. Not to mention Giulio, who should be given credit for mincing no words. In an impulse of kindness he acquiesced to doling out a small allowance to my offspring who were "still" his grandchildren, but I had to do the best I could with "what Sandro left me." What nerve!

Augusto arranged everything; how he did it I really don't know and was never curious enough to ask. I only know that in a few months he managed to settle unpaid bills with those crooks, because I think he was acquainted with some of the usurers and got the interest reduced in exchange for some past favor . . . that's all I know. All that was important to me was not to have anything to do with certain people ever again.

You know how it is: at the spin of the wheel of fate people turn their backs. The most absurd rumors went around about Sandro's death and my relationship with Augusto. Someone even suspected we had killed him. Sure, I thought, to pocket the fabulous inheritance!

Those who were a little better informed maintained that after all I had been fortunate, that Castaldi was the ideal catch, from a well-off family — "Yes, all right, he's from a class of newly rich peasants, but she can't be too choosy!" — "besides, you know how young people are: naive, passionate, and terribly ambitious . . ."

❖

Let them talk all they please, I thought, why should I waste my
breath when it was plain there was nothing left for me in Trieste?

I wasn't bothered by Dolly's breaking her engagement. After
all it was her life, and if she was so anxious to go off to be a servant
I wouldn't stand in her way.

I had other things to think about: finding a place to live.

Someplace for my two sons and me.

Actually I had little choice, and so we moved to Venice with my
sister. Those months would have been awful without visits from
Augusto, who at that time worked for a firm in Padua. I think I
would have gone completely mad, trapped as I was in that suffocating rabbinic environment.

We took walks through the narrow little Venetian streets, free
now to say and do as we pleased, and perhaps just for that reason
we felt strangely awkward and ill at ease.

I know it's hard to believe, but during all that time not once,
not one time, did Augusto take advantage of my precarious situation to importune me or make me feel uncomfortable. He waited
patiently. Sure of himself, probably, that I don't deny — and why
shouldn't he have been? We both knew we were too much alike
to remain separated for long.

As soon as we dared talk about marriage all hell broke loose. My
sister, aware of the fact that I would not hesitate a moment to
marry a "gentile," began to shout and cry like a madwoman. You
can't do this to our family. You can't pile such a shame on top of so
many other misfortunes. I was selfish, ungrateful, and didn't I
think about the boys? "Poor thing, you are still living in the Middle
Ages," I replied, confident that the Castaldis would greet the news
with a little more enthusiasm. But instead even Augusto had his
difficulties. The Castaldis' objections were, to tell the truth, decid-
edly more concrete: such as, I was too "old," I had three grown
children and a . . . somewhat dubious . . . past. They thought I was
not to be relied on, in other words. They insisted on believing that
I came from "too high" a society, that after all they were country

people. They had been fortunate, true enough, but they had always been simple people and it wouldn't do to go mixing with those who belonged to such a different world. "Sooner or later you'll find out at your own expense," they said . . .

Augusto didn't allow himself a moment's peace. I tried to calm him, restraining my annoyance as best I could: "They are suspicious, of course, reasoning like peasants. What can you expect?"

We married after a year, in the Venice Town Hall with few people and little festivity, but convinced in our hearts that our marriage would surprise them all, and that soon they would be forced to change their minds about us.

Goodness, how proud I was when we first started going out together! I certainly couldn't miss those sly and envious glances; but to be honest, I was glad to discover how scandalized they still were about the difference in our age, circumstances, backgrounds . . .

If I had had a choice, obviously I would never have moved to Pisa, but after so much wandering I reached the conclusion that one place was as good as another. How many houses, how many cities, and how many countries had I already lived in during my lifetime? And what was left of all of it?

How strange, though! I had lost everything, and yet I felt strong, charged with enthusiasm. I had a young man full of ambition by my side. After years of nothing but devastation, the idea of having to start all over filled me with marvelous energy instead of frightening me.

I know that many judged us excessive. Our euphoria, our vitality, and the will to enjoy ourselves seemed "exaggerated." We never missed a chance to go out to dance or play cards. We liked the same things; we laughed at the same jokes. We strolled through the downtown streets. I stopped in front of store windows, certain that the next day I would find on my bed the object that had attracted my attention. "You are completely out of your mind," I would say as I unwrapped his latest gift. And he would break out laughing with Titti, who was stationed by the door to enjoy seeing that spark of happiness shine in my eyes.

A day didn't go by that he didn't invent some new surprise, and I knew when he was getting something ready because his mouth would take on a curious smirk that he couldn't hide, a kind of half smile that always gave him away. There were not only presents, but also trips, invitations to dinner, spur-of-the-moment gatherings with friends I hadn't seen for months, hunting parties, garden concerts . . . One summer morning he drove up to the villa at Marina di Pisa in the latest-model Minerva. "It's for Dolly," he announced triumphantly, and Dolly, the idiot, flew off the handle instead of saying thank you. So in the end we kept the car ourselves. And then, because we didn't know how to drive, we naturally had to hire a driver.

We lived in a beautiful palazzo downtown, with a small but very well-tended garden. I had never had so many servants at my beck and call and I kept telling Augusto that maybe there were too many, that after all four maids weren't necessary, especially since Titti had started going to school. But then I dropped the subject. As Augusto's firm was rather well known and his clients very numerous, what difference could one servant more or less make?

It was the time of Mussolini. Moishele, as they called him in Trieste and as Marcello always said. I can't say why I liked him so much. It might have been his strength, his boldness, his virile ways. Anyway, I don't understand politics. He certainly knew how to talk to people, and he knew how to arouse enthusiasm. When there was a fascist meeting, with all those uniforms, I was moved, to tell the truth. Nothing had ever worked me up so much. And then I heard Augusto praise him to the skies, and he knew something about politics. When he was with people who didn't think as he did, he warmed up to the subject with such passion and overpowering determination that it didn't take him long to convince everyone.

Dora kept telling me that Augusto was my fourth child, and instead of making me mad, it made me almost proud — perhaps because it was a bit true: Augusto liked to play, laugh, joke. He was capable of doing the wildest things on the spur of the moment, and would be offended like a little boy if he were crossed. But he could also be very serious when dealing with a problem at work or planning the children's future. He was very fond of all of them, even Marcello, as strange as that may seem.

Augusto never talked about Marcello's "problem." He only hinted at his "character to toughen up" and his "refined intelligence" that would be "apt for service to the state," and I would look at him tenderly because I knew that nothing good would ever come from that boy, but I was happy that my husband still had some illusions.

Marcello, on the other hand, had immediately discovered Augusto's weak point and slyly attacked him. Trying to humiliate him had become his favorite pastime, the only one he allowed himself in his rare moments of lucidity. At the table he would systematically bring up our old Triestine friends, all people who were never important to him, but whom he mentioned for their high-sounding names, or in order to recount episodes from his childhood, such as the time Sandro put him on King Abbas's knees. "Where were we, Mama? Oh, yes, at Console Bayring's house! But do you know, Augusto, that he actually refused to become minister of foreign affairs . . . You should read his book . . . what is the title . . . Oh, yes, *Modern Egypt* . . . Oh, my goodness, excuse me. I forgot you don't know English."

Augusto never reacted, and I always wondered if he did it to preserve the peace and quiet or out of goodness . . .

That death was a welcome release for Marcello is indisputable. I have always thought: that boy never had a crumb of happiness, except perhaps in his early childhood when we were in Cairo, and yet . . . even there . . .

When I made such comments, Augusto would fly into a rage. I never understood whether he was angry with me or with himself for being "unable to save him." To save Marcello from his plan of destruction was a goal that could occur only to someone who had known him superficially.

After Marcello's death things in Pisa were definitely not the same. I was used to certain reactions by then and knew not to expect anything from such a provincial environment. Augusto, quite the opposite, felt uncomfortable, irritable, offended by those looks that were somewhere between pitying and scandalized.

Honestly, with all that happened afterward, I'm no longer so sure it was really Marcello's death that provoked those changes. The fact remains that from then on Augusto got it into his head that our life in Pisa was unsuitable for me, that I was accustomed to something quite different, that he wouldn't be satisfied until he was able to offer me the life I deserved and other such absurdities. He could talk of nothing else; it had become an obsession. And with all the problems we had I couldn't understand why he continued to insist so stubbornly on such nonsense: why should I care what the pharmacist or notary thought?

"See, that's the point. The pharmacist and notary aren't important to you because you are used to being with people of another caliber. Yes, my dear, an entirely different caliber . . ." Oh, God, I thought, there's no hope . . .

Actually, I was well aware that there was something else, a source of anxiety that escaped me, something that had to do just with Augusto that I couldn't grasp. I looked at him, watched him, searching for a sign. Nothing. He was always affable, kind, went everywhere with me. It's true he was working less. Who knows, I thought, perhaps he is annoyed about that time I told him not to be like Sandro, who always left me alone because of work . . . It was a joke, but I had to be careful with Augusto. He didn't like jokes having to do with my past. He didn't want to hear about it, as one doesn't want to be reminded of something threatening.

When we were with company, then, his nervousness reflected the palpable tension of those around us: I caught winks, looks of embarrassment, especially in the homes of certain friends of his, members of the literary circle Augusto had joined a few months before Marcello's death: "In order to put an end to the gossip that my wife's more cultured than I am," as he laughingly put it.

"I don't understand why Alfonsina stopped inviting us to René's concerts. We've always been very friendly with her."

"My darling, Pisa is so terribly provincial."

"What does that have to do with it? Until a few months ago we had a great time."

"They haven't changed, my dear; you've changed. It's simply that you are bored and don't want to admit it."

I don't remember exactly when the situation came to a head. I only know that one evening he came home fuming, confused, muttering incomprehensibly. According to him it was impossible to keep an office in Pisa. We had to return to Padua, where his father had bought us a house. That way we would be well settled, nearer my family. It would be better for everyone, because Pisa was a gray, miserable city and the Pisans small-minded people who did nothing but bad-mouth others. Better to leave, go to Padua, because my reputation came first before everything else . . . It was undoubtedly the right solution.

A contrived solution, I would cruelly discover after the move, and I have never forgiven him for manipulating me like that without finding the courage to tell me how things stood. And I an idiot who noticed nothing! When I think back over all those evenings at the "literary circle," the looks, and his stubborn insistence in attributing to me our friends' changed behavior . . . In only two months Augusto's losses at the casino in Viareggio were enough to force him to mortgage his office. I was never able to find out how long this had been going on. The only sure thing is that everyone else knew: friends, family, everyone. How I swallowed that mountain of lies! I really thought he wanted the house in Padua to make me happy, to be closer to places where I grew up. And the shame, the shame of discovering that his father was paying for everything, even for the servants, because Augusto hadn't worked in months!

The agreement with his father entailed, on his father's part, the cost of the house and servants. In exchange, we had to drastically change our lifestyle: no more surprise trips or senseless gifts, and above all no more "games," as Augusto liked to call them.

I was ready for anything just to get out of that nightmare. I had to think of Titti, and I couldn't permit another disaster. I had to find a way to set things straight. I told Augusto that I accepted the agreement without conditions, and I also told him that I was willing to forgive him. I needed him.

I don't know what Augusto was thinking. In his stupor he seemed already resigned to the idea of my disappearing forever from his life. He looked at me bewildered, moved, with a mixture of shame and pride, as if my saying I couldn't manage without him had shaken him up. And I thought: but for heaven's sake, how can he think I would leave him? Leave him to go where?

He began to work enthusiastically; he swore that everything would be different, that he had "reformed for Our good." I don't know if I believed him or not, but I had to trust him. I thought: who of us hasn't made a mistake in his life? And I certainly wasn't the right person to reproach him for his gambling obsession . . .

Fortunately for me, the period of Augusto's "reformation" coincided with my Titti's entry into the Avanguardisti.

Those photographs . . . I will never tire of looking at them: my darling standing next to the flag in knickerbockers and his fez slightly tipped to the right. He always posed like that: one hand on his hip and the other, in a black leather glove, to his side. The tight sash at his waist emphasized his slender figure, perfect for the uniform.

That uniform had become a real fixation for my Nacci. He wore it everywhere, even around the house, and Augusto teased him by calling him "little Narcissus."

❖

Dolly didn't come down off her mountains very often to visit us, but on the rare occasions when she did, she didn't waste any time asking Titti to change his clothes. How angry she made me . . . why should she care, I thought, if it makes him happy. What does it matter to her if he wants to go around dressed like that from morning to night!

Actually, Titti didn't seem to care, or if it hurt him he didn't let on. He often came home late after a meeting, and when I worried about him, Augusto would give me a sidelong glance, scolding me with a smile: "Look, he's a man now. A man ready to give his life for his country." Oh, goodness me, let's hope he doesn't get such foolish ideas in his head. It's enough that his father ruined the family for his country . . .

Of all my children, Titti was the only one I couldn't bear the thought of his leaving me. "He must always stay home, even if he gets married," I told Augusto. "We'll find a large house and he can always stay with us." In fact, to tell the truth, one of the few things about fascism I didn't like was that insistence on tearing children from their mothers to send them to those silly military camps.

The day the postcard arrived announcing the summer camp I begged Augusto to do something, and he arranged for my Nacci to enter the Alpine Corp of Montenero d'Istria, where we knew he would be treated well by Colonel Montalcini. Every two days I received a short note with some affectionate and comforting words. I would read it and reread it under Augusto's exasperated gaze. I wrote him at least two letters a day. Not that I had much to say, but it gave me the illusion of having him closer. I had suddenly felt a longing for certain people and places, a vague sense of emptiness . . . nothing actually concrete, just a little melancholy for the passing of time. The three of us had now formed a kind of family and that house seemed empty without my Titti. But Augusto didn't want to hear about such things. He took my every mood like a personal offense and I began to tire of his insecurities. Wasn't I allowed even a moment's uneasiness without feeling the need to justify myself? What could he know about the feelings of a forty-four-year-old woman on the brink of losing the last thread that tied her to her youth?

At the end of that summer, after Marina di Pisa, I decided to spend a few weeks at the Lido to be with my sister and those few Triestine friends I had stayed in contact with. At the sea I still swam a lot, and even if my energy was no longer what it once was, I managed well enough. Augusto would accompany me, but he felt uncomfortable. He wasn't like Sandro and Marcello, who pretended not to like the sea just to strike an attitude. The problem was that Augusto didn't know how to swim and didn't want the others to find out.

Actually, it was the first time since we were married that we spent a little time with people of "my world." That world had a devastating effect on Augusto. He felt he was being judged. He entered into a permanent state of tension that threw him completely off kilter: his verve turned into confusion. He was unable to express his thoughts clearly, and the harder he tried, the more incoherent he became.

It embarrassed me no end! Anyone would have been embarrassed dealing with his sudden metamorphosis. I tried, without success, to explain that my friends weren't there to pillory him, and that he didn't have to prove anything to anyone. But he didn't believe me, and not because I wasn't convincing. The truth is he took pleasure in it: for some incomprehensible reason he liked to think that everyone was looking down on him.

In the beginning he showed his change in imperceptible ways, little insignificant remarks. Then he started giving more frequent signs of irritation. He often found fault with me, became impatient, picked quarrels about everything. I've never liked to quarrel. I've always thought it vulgar. So, when he took that ugly turn, I would go for a walk and wait for it to pass. When I returned home, sometimes after several hours, I would find him humbled, ready to do anything for my forgiveness, with such a sincere and disarming air it was impossible to resist.

❖

Then there was the bill with Calamai, my tailor in Florence. Two checks were returned because they were not covered. I thought it was a mistake . . . I asked Augusto for an explanation. He dodged my questions with the excuse of a work appointment. I didn't know what to do and was very ashamed, as I had never let a debt go unpaid.

One by one all the checks began to bounce, until the tradesmen politely let me know that they preferred to be paid in cash.

Augusto was a man of principles. His life, his way of behavior, could be summarized in a handful of precepts that he respected scrupulously. Among them one served as his absolute foundation stone: attack is the best defense . . .

"Do you know what amazes me the most? It's that you always seem to agree with everyone. Whatever anyone says to you, you always find the correct, brilliant reply, so tailored to any situation that it's impossible to know what you really think."

He would speak without looking at me; or I should say, he would look at me sideways just as Marcello did. The same look in his eyes, the same smell in the house. The same wish to punish the only unavoidable witness to his self-destruction.

Exactly when he began I don't know. I only know that very soon he stopped even pretending to keep it secret. His "little smokes" became more and more frequent, and the more frequent they were, the less control he had.

"Do you see how beautiful Gemma is this evening? But of course, it's impossible not to notice. And in fact our dear Modigliani can't take his eyes off her."

"Darling, the sincere interest in your wife's trivial conversation on the part of a man like Signor Modigliani can only flatter us both."

"Ha, ha! Very good, my dear. I've always admired your ability to turn every situation to your advantage."

At dinner parties everyone laughed when he acted that way. No one seemed to notice how brutally honest he was being at those times.

How long had we been married? Three years, I believe.
Oh, Lord, how quickly things turn around . . .

By now Titti didn't stay home much, as was normal for a boy his age . . . and besides I encouraged him to go out because I thought it was better that way. I didn't want him to notice anything, and I think I succeeded for a while. I remember when he got off the train after the summer camp. The crowd on the platform, the engine smoke, and those boys in uniform who all looked alike: I was so confused that I didn't recognize him — and not because he was taller, because he had been full grown for some time. He had become a man, and his face, with that very short hair and dark sunburned skin, seemed thinner and more defined. He had never been so handsome. And as I stood there admiring him, dazed and awestruck, he laughed with his friends. "Look at her, it's like she's seeing me for the first time!"

Augusto was very good about saving appearances. If he knew that there was a dinner party he was always impeccable, elegant, clear-headed, with that sure manner that could still win me over. When he realized that his aggressiveness toward me didn't help his image, he became more careful about staying off opium before certain occasions. On the other hand, if we had no plans, I would find him stretched out on the bed in a dressing gown with a satisfied expression — never dazed, however, but calm, nothing like Marcello . . .

Opium works like this: one begins by smoking ten, then slowly, inexorably works up to twenty, then fifty, sixty, and so on. But not at once: slowly, month after month. For a while the situation seems under control until one fine day it suddenly takes over. Then, in order to feel decent, Augusto had to smoke more than ninety pipes a day. No use talking about work, obviously.

How many times, after it was all over, I've been asked: "Why didn't you ever talk with someone? Why didn't you get some help?" But whom should I have talked to, for heaven's sake! And it had nothing to do with shame — would that it were the first time! — it's just that no one would have believed a story like that. No one but his family. And what help could I have received from those wealthy clodhoppers who would have undoubtedly accused me of making him lapse back in the vice after they had "cured" him. They "cured" him by sending him to the same sanatorium as Marcello. But opium was more insidious than morphine, more widespread socially, and easier to hide. And how can they be sure he ever really stopped? I was certainly not sure of anything anymore, especially after learning from the accountant that the Castaldis hadn't paid us a lira for at least three months. Not one red cent.

Titti was so sweet and thoughtful during that time . . . He tried to console me by saying that if Augusto "weren't well," he would look after me. How sweet to offer to become his mother's cavalier when it would have been more than right for him to go enjoy himself with his friends! He went with me to performances and dinner parties. And the pride of having that magnificent boy by my side helped distract my thoughts for a while from that phantasm of a man that we had left at home.

When he saw us go out together, Augusto always seemed irritated. I don't think he was jealous, but envious, rather . . . Titti usually waited for me at the bottom of the stairs, elegant and smiling, and I would kiss him, fix a button, smooth out a wrinkle, or straighten his collar.

"But don't you see that he is a man now and you are embarrassing him?"

"It seems to me you're the only one who's embarrassed."

Every once in a while Augusto would come to my room and watch me at the dressing table. He would lean against the doorway, ready to spit out comments, but his tone was caressing now, calm, without the slightest trace of aggression.

"How clever you are to always stay so perfect while everything is collapsing around you. The right woman at the right time, who adapts herself to everyone she talks to and to every situation. Who speaks a different language with everyone. A different language, yes . . . but still, with everyone."

Then it happened that they called him to Ferrara for an important political meeting. At least that's what he said, and it was undoubtedly the truth since his comrades confirmed that fact after what happened. Who knows, I thought, perhaps they found out about his vice and want to warn him. It would be a good thing, because perhaps they are the only ones able to talk sense to him. When he left I was very pleased. I knew the influence that certain people had over him, and besides he was very well acquainted with the head of the party at Ferrara, who would certainly scold him as one scolds a son because, after all, he had gone too far, and his behavior was beginning to be an embarrassment even for the party's good image.

He had to be away for two days, and he told me that he would telephone the first evening. Instead, not a word. But I didn't worry. He had probably gone to supper with someone and had forgotten to call me.

After four days Dolly arrived. I don't know why. Well, yes, it was Nacci who asked her to come. He thought I would be happy to have her with me. Poor boy, he was so good that he couldn't imagine certain things.

Dolly seemed worried. Of course I didn't open my mouth around her. Why would I confide in someone who always considered me the cause of every bad thing that happened? On the other hand, I was sure by the way she looked at me that Titti had told her more than he should. I'm convinced he hadn't done it maliciously. How could he imagine that for his sister all this merely confirmed my wickedness? Dolly had already drawn her own conclusions, as I could see by the slightly scornful looks she gave me: see how Mama has made Augusto revert to dependence because of her foolishness. She made him miserable, just as she had made Marcello miserable before him, and that poor fellow took refuge in an artificial paradise in order to escape her.

For Dolly it was a kind of revenge. Like something out of a cheap novel, certainly, but revenge just the same.

I never found out what really happened. I only know that the evening before his disappearance, Augusto had arrived at the meeting in an agitated state. His comrades who were there told me. It seems that when he went to the house of G___ he had the impression someone was following him and he was very nervous. That night he stayed in a place he knew on the banks of the Po. According to the owners he seemed in a good enough mood, a little distracted, perhaps, but calm. And then, when the police finally fished him out of the river, where were his documents and wallet? And his head wound? Yes, all right, it could have happened when he fell, but what if they had hit him and thrown him off the bridge? The last person who saw him that morning said he was sitting on the bank eating a bunch of grapes. But does someone eat a bunch of grapes before killing himself?

TITTI

*W*HAT A SAD WEDDING ...
She beautiful, hieratic, almost frightened. He awkward, every gesture seemed an apology. At the last moment nearly all the family members were absent, suddenly afflicted by some kind of flu. There were only her faithful friends, the few who refused to hold that couple responsible for my father's death ... Dolly and Marcello stood close to each other, united, accomplices as always, especially when it came to passing judgment on Mama. I had overcome my mistrust — not because Augusto had won me over in some way, but I saw that my mother was so happy and carefree that I had to be grateful to that man, whatever his fault in regard to our family. I was still a boy. I looked at the world differently, and Marcello was right when he said that I loved everyone. It was my greatest defect, if that's the right word for it. I forgave easily because I didn't want to believe in wickedness, and perhaps that is why I have always been the only one to look on Gemma's many false steps with indulgence and tenderness.

Immediately after Papa's death we moved to Venice, but our personal belongings were still dispersed between the Villa delle Rose and our grandparents' house in Trieste. Sorting things out was painful only for Mama. Dolly, Marcello, and I couldn't be bothered with it. The only thing that made me really sad was to see how upset Gemma was after Grandfather Giulio's visits; that man judged her harshly without any compromise.

The Levis decided that Mama should return everything that came from their family. A contemptible thing, thinking back over it, but one that Gemma accepted without argument. It seems that Papa had left many debts and Mama hoped it would help Giulio settle them. Once this last business that still tied us to my father's family was taken care of, we moved to Pisa for a short while, just long enough for Marcello to figure out that there was no use in his hanging around any longer.

My first memories after my brother's death are the times spent in Padua, at Villa Castaldi. I took an immediate liking to that city. In the mornings at dawn I would go on my bicycle along the fog-covered canals with my dog Picchio, trying to ease my pain over those deaths on the solitary rides. Mama and Castaldi were all I had left, like it or not.

In less than three years I had lost the two men I had grown up with — a rather brutal way to enter adolescence. I was so mixed up and bewildered that I was bound to grab at whatever could provide a little security. I needed to feel affection for a dependable person who would never abandon me, and Augusto now gave me his full attention. Until then all his energy had gone to Marcello and his improbable future, and now he was concerned about me, felt compassion for me, wanted to renew my faith and help me recover the enthusiasm of my age.

However, it wasn't he who talked me into fascism, or indoctrinated me — as Dolly said. It wasn't necessary; it was something one felt in the air, something a fourteen-year-old couldn't resist.

Augusto and those around him had my full attention: first his friends, and then his "comrades." I never tired of hearing them talk about the great changes that Il Duce had carried out, and yet mine was not simple admiration: it was the faith, the will to believe I was absolutely safe.

Suddenly it was decided that I, who had always been taught at home by tutors, should be sent to school to acquire the "comradely" spirit. Not another word was mentioned about bar mitzvah or Hebrew lessons. Contrary to what others believed, I never thought that that choice was a consequence of fascist "indoctrination" or of a "gentile" marrying into the family. I simply believe that Mama, having no more responsibility toward the Levis, finally felt free to raise me as she felt best, without having to answer to anyone. Whatever the reason, the main thing for me was finally getting out of the house and seeing the world. A world in which I felt for the first time that I had my own space and friends for exchanging ideas and points of view. I was entering adulthood and that is the way I satisfied my need for belonging, by constructing a new family inside and outside the house.

And besides (I freely admit it), I liked Augusto. Not because he was "fascinating" or "cultured," as I often heard it said, but just the opposite. He seemed to me to be more than anything a simple person, almost a little crude, tremendously tender and impulsive in everything he did. He was fond of me, and even if he sometimes showed it in a clumsy way, pretending an understanding and complicity that some would have found pathetic, I saw in his conduct only the desperate need to make himself liked. I was certain that the deaths of my father and brother were a burden he couldn't shake off, and I thought I could help relieve his oppressive sense of guilt by giving him the way to show that, basically, he was a nice person. These reflections, naturally, I make only after the fact: at the time I limited myself to loving him as much as he loved me, without asking myself too many questions, without trying to give any special significance to our reciprocal need for affection and harmony.

❖

Dolly rarely came to see us, but — curiously — as much as I continued to miss her, in reality I could no longer stand her presence. The fact is that Dolly constituted a threat to that fragile and, all told, artificial equilibrium that we had patiently managed to create, and that's what I could no longer tolerate. To hear her speak with contempt, if not with pity, about my political activities, to catch her looks of irritation over my life choices and affections, couldn't leave me indifferent . . . I decided to reject that terrible influence she exercised over me in order to escape the memories and the need to make an accounting with the past. I felt propelled forward, pushed toward new challenges that I couldn't wait to face.

Whether aware if it or not, Augusto represented exactly what I needed at that moment. I, who had been surrounded by somber and suffering males throughout my childhood, could finally abandon myself to the pleasure of jokes, could laugh with that child-man who looked at everything with the superficiality and casualness of someone who didn't seem to know the existence of sorrow.

Every time he came home with one of his innumerable gifts, he was seized by a kind of frenzy in his impatience to watch us unwrap the surprise. He proudly observed our enthusiasm with the air of a child who has successfully recited a poem in public.

Dolly was right when she said that Augusto was not intelligent but instinctively bright. His smug jokes, his stock comments exasperated her. She found them "vulgar." I don't know what Dolly meant by vulgarity, but I believe that, like all those who belong to a certain set, she considered every direct, impulsive behavior unmediated by a certain form to be vulgar. But for me there was nothing more reassuring than Castaldi's spontaneity. In his way of doing things there was a sincerity that inspired trust. There could be no ambiguities, misunderstandings, or ulterior motives with him. Everything was clear and simple, even a little frivolous — I don't deny it. But so what?

❖

My devotion to fascism represented a period of naive exaltation based on the happiness, on the pleasure of being with a group; on finally feeling an integral part of a social structure. We were all children and we certainly had no big political ideas. What attracted us most of all was pride in wearing a uniform, of being able to act like adults, to conform with what was going on around us. My romantic patriotism found a reason for being, a pretext. And above all, I was enjoying myself. I entered the Avanguardisti just as soon as I reached the required age, encouraged by Mama and Augusto, whom I had finally quit calling Signor. On the day of the swearing-in ceremony Castaldi kept giving me advice and he looked at me with a father's pride, or rather, the pride of a man frustrated in his paternal desires.

It was obvious that Augusto had dreamed of having his own children, and he had certainly made quite a sacrifice by marrying Mama, since he knew it would put an end to that dream. And I also believe that's the reason he did all he could to make us like him and continued to take Marcello's death as a personal defeat. I sensed his wish to be liked and took a little advantage of it. We would talk over the positions taken by the party that we always accepted wholeheartedly — I out of laziness and he because of his practical sense. We would get as excited as two schoolboys, and, thinking back on it, I don't believe I ever turned to him as a father, but considered him more a companion, a special friend. He probably suffered from my inability to take him totally seriously.

Augusto urged me to make a career with the Avanguardisti, but my weak-willed nature led me to refuse any situation requiring commitment. It was all right as long as it was a matter of wearing the uniform and marching in parades. But my thinking didn't go beyond that.

It was different with Castaldi. He saw the regime as a way of improving his social and financial position. Augusto was without a doubt emblematic of the new ruling class that was establishing itself. Often those emerging figures were only the newly rich small bourgeoisie looked on with scorn by high society, but the fact remains that my mother had been excluded from that world, and the company that had previously seemed *déplacée* now represented to her the only possible way of existence.

My studies soon began to suffer from the obligations of my political activism, and although it was Castaldi who had encouraged me in that direction, he suddenly began to show signs of impatience.

His irritation was due in large part to the fact that Mama was upset with him every time I came home with a bad grade, accusing him of having "ruined my brain." As if that weren't enough, she often made allusions to the attention Father had always given to our education, and I can't forget the effect that kind of remark had on Augusto. Gemma didn't notice, but the perverse dynamics that were being created between her and her husband were now obvious: Mama became ever more intolerant of certain company they kept and Castaldi didn't feel he was in the position to offer her the refinements of life she once had. I'm sure Mama was never aware of his frustration. She never would have admitted feeling nostalgia for the world that had so mercilessly shoved her aside, but both Castaldi and I knew her well enough to be conscious of her dissatisfactions.

Dolly's visits to Marina di Pisa grew shorter and shorter. She insisted that after Marcello's death she couldn't come back to that beach, but I knew what she really couldn't abide was seeing what "I had become." I'm sorry Dolly was never able to understand my youthful impulse, that her stubborn nature never allowed her to find the necessary tolerance. Who knows, perhaps one day she too will learn to look at the world in a more kindly light . . .

I was growing up and I knew that people were beginning to say that I was "a handsome young man." Mama observed me with a mixture of apprehension and amazement, proud to see that I was becoming a man, but also alarmed at the idea that I might soon be out of her clutches. The Avanguardisti kept me constantly on the go — camps, training, maneuvers — and these occasions fueled Gemma's anxiety. Thanks to the recommendations of some of Augusto's acquaintances, I was even assigned to a regiment where she knew I would be given special consideration. I often asked myself if the passage to adulthood isn't in some way commensurate with the increased irritation provoked by one's parents. It certainly was that way with me. What I would have taken as a wonderful affectionate act the day before suddenly assumed the form of aggression. No matter how hard I tried to prove it to others, I realized that I was and would always be someone of privilege. I fooled myself that I had become an integral part of a group, on a par with my comrades, but I discovered that actually I had always been a spoiled baby who at the most had been granted the luxury of an adventure.

During the months away at summer camp I had no clue about what was going on at home. Mama sent me trite postcards, and even though I knew that writing was not her forte, the infantile style of her communications never ceased to amaze me.

Anyway, my thoughts were projected elsewhere. No longer toward the military demands that were beginning to bore me: my thoughts were now turned in another direction entirely . . .

Her name was Lydia. I met her a month before leaving for camp and I couldn't wait to see her again.

I remember my return home as a deep rupture. And it wasn't due only to my entrance into the adult stage of my life; I seemed to see everything in a new light. I felt detached, as though disconnected from the familial universe that had been my point of reference up to that time. Augusto's "depression" was full blown: all that remained of the slightly arrogant young man, vain and full of himself, was a helpless being, a chipped vase showing all its cracks. I wasn't as disappointed as I was amazed. Contrary to what many people had believed, and certainly what Dolly believed, I had never put great hopes in Augusto. I was fond of him, just as one is fond of a family member, nothing more. Thus, the only feeling I could muster was surprise: how had this person, apparently the most transparent and linear being I had ever met, hidden such a profound malaise behind his bravado?

And then Mama, suddenly so old . . .

It had happened overnight: first her hair, then her face, the subtle wrinkles growing thicker, the slower movements, her body as though shifting its axis . . . She deluded herself that she could hide her physical deterioration, and her anxiety, behind forced activity, but I knew her well enough to know that her spells of overexcitement were a bad omen. She seemed different, no longer in control of herself, and — I'm ashamed to admit it — she began to embarrass me.

I went out often — encouraged by Mother, strangely enough. It should have made me suspicious: she who was usually so possessive now no longer held me back. I asked her what was wrong with Augusto and she said he didn't feel very well, or that he was busy writing who knows what speech: "You mustn't go into his room because you'll break his concentration. Go out with your friends, enjoy yourself, don't worry about us . . ."

The fact is I didn't worry about them. I guessed, I knew, but I had no wish to hear how things really were with them.

". . . I don't understand, Signor Castaldi. What are you referring to?"

Gemma was on the telephone in the hall and I was getting ready to go out.

I stopped, not wanting her to see me. I didn't want to have to explain what I did each day.

The silence went on for a long while and Gemma — usually so bold with Augusto's father — spoke with a trembling voice: "I have no idea what you are talking about. Augusto hasn't told me anything. I thought they were bills . . ."

Silence. Through the frosted-glass door I could perceive only her figure suddenly bent over: "I don't understand why you say these things . . . so . . . vulgar . . . I've done all I can do. It's just that he doesn't want to listen to reason. Perhaps you could . . ."

The communication was interrupted. I don't know if voluntarily or by whom. I only know that I decided to retreat silently to my room in order not to have to face that woman grappling with the latest of her many setbacks.

To soothe my sense of guilt I had begun going out with Mama. "If Augusto doesn't feel well, let me distract you a little." I must shamefully confess that actually I was taking advantage of her presence at my side in order to meet Lydia without arousing suspicion. Those outings, however, did little to distract Gemma, and the more she seemed engrossed in her own thoughts, the more I acted happy and carefree to discourage her confidences. I will always regret my insensitive refusal to help her. I'm not trying to make excuses. The fact is that I felt trapped, exasperated by her irrepressible disposition for provoking disaster . . . I, Titti, the one she loved and had always loved the most. But there are circumstances where love doesn't mean anything anymore: not if it causes pain, not if it is powerless. And that was the only brief moment in my life when my mother's love, instead of giving me strength, was transformed into an intolerable burden.

I became very skilled at avoiding risky situations. It was not all that difficult, since the chance of my seeing Augusto and Gemma together became less and less likely. The first objective of each day was to steer clear of the Castaldi couple. However, there were unavoidable occasions, such as Sunday dinner, during which, for some unfathomable reason, Augusto was invariably present and always fairly lucid.

Opium abuse had spared nothing but Castaldi's worst characteristics. It was as though the screen behind which he had contrived to hide himself for years had cruelly collapsed. He reminded me of a robot I had as a child, when its mechanism was suddenly broken. It sat in the middle of the dresser, still polished and well dressed, but its movements were erratic and out of control, and it seemed to enjoy the devastating effects of its wild inner works.

Actually they both behaved in an exasperating way: Mama

dressed and acted like an impoverished aristocrat; he seemed the caricature of a provincial fascist party leader, devoured by insecurities, by a sense of inadequacy in comparison with his wife, his parents, with life. He exhibited his complexes with a braggadocio and an aggressiveness that hindered any efforts of communication: he had lost his panache and without that Augusto was nothing . . .

It took Gemma's sobbing to make me react. I had never seen Gemma cry — not for Papa's death, not for Marcello's. She sobbed in frustration as she frantically rummaged through overcoat pockets in a desperate search for money. It was those sudden, unexpected, incongruous tears that made me face the facts.

I was panic-stricken. I wrote Dolly to come as soon as possible. I needed her impassiveness, her practical sense. Only she would be able to stop that vortex. I felt completely bewildered, frightened, convinced that there was something supernatural in Mama's ability to bring out the dark side of those near her . . .

The last conversation with Augusto before his disappearance was along the Brenta Naviglio. It was raining and he had turned up his coat collar as protection from the wind. I had to take a book back to the library and for some reason he, who almost never went out anymore, offered to go along with me. We walked without looking at each other, heads down to shield ourselves from the torrential rain, but that wasn't the only reason.

For some time now we had given up political discussions. We couldn't even pretend an interest in it, so palpable was the other anxiety that gripped us. We attempted some vague reference to the Concordat, to my disappointing military experience, but we both knew that certainly wasn't what we wanted to talk about.

Yet neither of us could find the courage to face the subject. Augusto moved silently along the parapet and looked at the water flowing fast and impetuously, full of the sludge brought by the autumn rains: "All this mud . . . I wonder if it ends up in the sea . . ."

EPILOGUE

DOLLY

TITTI DIED OF PERITONITIS when he was twenty-two years old.

Gemma had to wait a long time before joining him.

On the nightstand beside her bed she left a blue envelope with my name on it. Inside was a folded slip of paper with the epitaph she wanted inscribed on her tomb:

> *Titti's mama, Gemma Tedeschi, widow Levi.*
> *Her tragic life ended, she rests beside him.*

VENICE REVEALED
An Intimate Portrait
by Paolo Barbaro

ROME AND A VILLA
Memoir
by Eleanor Clark

The Adventures of
PINOCCHIO
by Carlo Collodi

TORREGRECA
Life, Death, Miracles
by Ann Cornelisen

WOMEN OF THE SHADOWS
Wives and Mothers of Southern Italy
by Ann Cornelisen

THE TWENTY-THREE DAYS
OF THE CITY OF ALBA
by Beppe Fenoglio

ARTURO'S ISLAND
by Elsa Morante

HISTORY
by Elsa Morante

THE LIBRARIANS OF ALEXANDRIA
by Alessandra Lavagnino
(available March 2006)

THE WATCH
by Carlo Levi

THE CONFORMIST
by Alberto Moravia

THE TIME OF INDIFFERENCE
by Alberto Moravia

THE WOMAN OF ROME
by Alberto Moravia

TWO WOMEN
by Alberto Moravia

LIFE OF MORAVIA
by Alberto Moravia and Alain Elkann

Claudia Roden's
THE FOOD OF ITALY
Region by Region

CUCINA DI MAGRO
Cooking Lean the Traditional Italian Way
by G. Franco Romagnoli

CONCLAVE
by Roberto Pazzi

THE ABRUZZO TRILOGY
by Ignazio Silone

MY NAME,
A LIVING MEMORY
by Giorgio van Straten

LITTLE NOVELS OF SICILY
by Giovanni Verga

OPEN CITY
Seven Writers in Postwar Rome
edited by William Weaver